Ragdolled

by

Katja Desjarlais

Doll Parts, Book One

The Wild Rose Press, Inc.
PO Box 708
Adams Basin, NY 14410-0708
Visit us at www.thewildrosepress.com

Publishing History
First Edition, 2024
Trade Paperback ISBN 978-1-5092-5884-0
Digital ISBN 978-1-5092-5885-7

Doll Parts, Book One
Published in the United States of America

Dedication

For Costco, whose coffee fueled the writing and editing of this book

Chapter One

Malcolm

The first thing I notice when I step off the elevator is the corporate sign hanging high above the receptionists' desk, *Doll Parts* spelled out in white block letters on glossy black. It's simple. Elegant. Posh, in that unassuming way the poshest things are.

I don't know what I was expecting when I came here, but classy definitely wasn't it.

A tall peacock of a woman straightens beside a filing cabinet and greets me with the lift of one eyebrow, which disappears beneath her turquoise bangs. She's wearing a bright pink-and-green print dress and purple leggings. The colors border on assaulting to the senses but somehow work on her lean frame. Her eyes narrow as I approach her desk, her gaze scanning me over like I'm a show pony put to auction.

Which isn't far from the truth.

"If you're Malcolm Sullivan, you can sit," she orders, pointing a neon-yellow fingertip at a lone chair in the center of the room. "If you aren't, head right back down the elevator and fill out the online application. We don't take walk-ins."

I sit, itching to undo the top button of my shirt before it chokes me out and my unconscious body is pecked to death. Though with the amount of money I need by the end of August being so far out of reach, death might actually be less stressful.

"Yeah, I'm Malcolm. I have an interview at four o'clock?"

"Are you asking me or telling me?" the peacock demands, taking her place behind her desk and angling her laptop toward me, the screen filled with the requisite closeup photo I submitted on my application. "Because my schedule says I have Malcolm Sullivan at four o'clock, but this Malcolm Sullivan describes himself as confident, easy-going, and a natural conversationalist. You—" She pauses to look me over again, her perusal less appreciative than it was a moment ago. "—look as stressed, uncomfortable, and awkward as a prep school frat boy under interrogation by a cop not bought off with daddy's money."

And here I was thinking I look like a dick.

A smug one, at that.

The charcoal suit and white dress shirt were custom tailored for me long ago, one set of many I needed to keep the endorsements rolling in. My blond hair looks darker than usual with the shit I used to keep it slicked back, the waves tamed for now but waiting for one gust of wind to ruin the style. The tanned, freshly shaved look makes me appear younger than my twenty-five years, but it might work in my favor.

Except, according to the peacock, I look like an uptight moron who stumbled into the wrong interview.

Channeling every piece of advice my former publicist gave me back when I was someone, I force my shoulders to drop, my spine to relax, and my bouncing knee to still. A practiced smile replaces the frown I was donning moments ago, and I scan her desk for the tiny gold nameplate almost hidden by a photo of her in a wedding dress, a woman who looks like her polar opposite at her side in a tux.

"My apologies, Ms. Merchant. As you can see from the beach picture I submitted with my application, I'm significantly more comfortable out of shirts than in them. Especially when they're tight enough to cut off my airway."

The peacock chuckles and rights her laptop screen, her fingers flying across the keyboard. "Lovely. Another smartass. Let's begin, shall we?"

The questions come fast, a mixed bag aimed to judge my work ethic, view on women, and general personality, but none of them throw me until the end.

"Doll Parts prides itself on maintaining a quality product base, Mr. Sullivan. And while you have the looks, the personality, and the overall manners of a Doll Parts employee, we require more." She looks over her screen at me, her light-blue eyes hard. "What skills make you useful to our clientele, Mr. Sullivan?"

Giving in to the need for a lungful of air, I pop the top two buttons of my shirt. "Skills?"

"Skills, talents, abilities," Ms. Merchant states. "What is it about you that will make our clients request you, make them want to come back for more?"

I can feel the blood draining from my face, and it isn't heading south like it usually does when sex talk is on the table. Nope. This time I'm pretty sure I'm bleeding out across the black tiled floor because I can't do this.

But I can't afford not to either.

Clearing my throat, I adjust my position, clasping my hands as I hunch over my knees to stop myself from passing out or running for the exit. "Well, um, I'm pierced in a few places and do this thing with my tongue—"

Her cackle rings through the room, reverberating off the walls. "Oh my sweet summer child," she says with a sigh. "God, I wish they were all as darling as you. No, honey. We don't peddle sex here. By 'skills,' I mean what can you offer? Our catalogue includes handymen, mechanics, dancers, tennis players, landscapers…you name it, we aim to provide it. Yes, some of our clients are looking for dates to events and dinner companions, but here at Doll Parts, Adrian Dawson has built an empire in providing much more. Our employees go car shopping and train for marathons. They serve as ballroom dance partners and golf companions. One specializes in video games and is booked for the next three months solid." Her razor-thin brows furrow. "Are you a gamer? We could use another to meet demand."

I blink as I straighten up and rack my brain for anything that might give me an edge without causing my worlds to collide. "I don't game, but, uh—"

"Naturally, financial compensation is increased for skilled bookings," she continues, misreading my hesitation. "The standard charge is two hundred dollars per hour with a minimum of a four-hour booking, but that price increases to three hundred per hour for skilled bookings. Clients are responsible for all expenses, but transportation is on you within a fifty-mile radius. After Doll Parts receives its standard twenty-five percent cut, your profit margin will be significantly higher than those of our competitors."

Three hundred dollars per hour.

It's not competition win money, and it sure as hell

isn't endorsement level, but given my options of this or becoming king of the caramel macchiato down on the boardwalk for a fraction of that, my decision is made.

"I surf," I state, my damaged knee sending a warning shot of pain through me. "So I guess anything water related would be my thing."

For the first time since I stepped off the elevator, Ms. Merchant looks interested. "Are you any good?"

The best, I almost reply before I catch myself and mentally shake off the borderline delusional proclamation. "I'm decent on a board."

Decent.

The word makes my buttoned collar feel ten sizes too small, the jacket constricting my chest as I shove the reminder of what I was aside and focus on what I am now. "I can do swim lessons, boarding, boogie boards, anything in the ocean or in a pool."

"Love it," she replies with a serpentine smile, her yellow nails tapping away on her computer. "We don't have any guys filling that niche, so I wouldn't be surprised if your initial time slots fill quickly with clients curious about getting into the water with you." She gives me another of those full-body scans, which feels weirdly clinical and not one bit lecherous. "With any luck, you'll have enough skill to keep them coming back for more. Any other talents that don't involve the water?"

Swallowing, I shake my head because I have nothing else. Surfing was all I ever wanted to do, all I ever did. "Nope."

Seemingly satisfied, Ms. Merchant stands and walks around her desk and handed me a manilla envelope stuffed with papers. "Your background check and medical records came back clear, as well as your driving record. Check your messages in an hour, download the Doll Parts app, and log in using the password in the email. All your appointments and info will be there, as well as rules, expectations, and directions. There's a probationary period of two months. We'll need these back before your first booking, which may be as soon as Friday. Pay extra attention to the benefits package and sign everywhere you find a blue sticky note."

Nodding, I give her a tight smile, still on the fence about how I'm feeling about the idea of renting myself out to random women even if sex isn't on the table. "I'll be back tomorrow with everything."

Ms. Merchant grins, and while I think she's trying to be reassuring, it's more than a little terrifying because I swear I see dollar signs in her pupils.

"I hope so, Mr. Sullivan. I have a feeling this little surfing hobby of yours is going to make you a hot commodity."

****

Malcolm
One Week Later

"I don't know what the fuck I was thinking." I groan, grabbing a towel out of my bag to wipe down my board and tossing another over to Jeremiah, my best friend and former competition. "Tonight's going to be a goddamn disaster."

He scrubs the towel over his short brown hair and laughs. Laughs. Like I'm not freaking the hell out enough as it is.

"What, you scared you're going to be stuck being on the receiving end of some eighty-year-old woman's game of grabass? Maybe you'll luck out and it'll be some smokin' married cougar with daddy issues and a platinum card."

I hike my board under my arm and start the short trek to my apartment. "Seriously? You're gonna go there?"

He winces. "Ah hell, Cole. I wasn't thinking." He scans the street for cars, then jogs alongside me until we hit the sidewalk. "But come on. You have to know what kind of women you're going to be meeting working this kind of job."

"Doll Parts isn't an escort service," I grumble, unlocking my door and sliding my board onto a set of the hooks I installed when I moved in. Jeremiah does the same as I grab two waters from the fridge and hand one over. "In fact, they have three pages of rules about touching and a million warnings about accepting money for sex. I'm just, like, a companion."

He downs half a bottle in one gulp. "Companion has a lot of room for interpretation. What'll you do when one of these chicks slaps down a thousand bucks and asks to be fucked ten ways from Sunday?"

Choking on my drink, I cough until a hand slams against my back a few times. "Jeez," I sputter, gripping the edge of the small island. "I don't know, okay? I say no. This gig pays well enough that I might actually be able to pull this buy off by the deadline without getting my dick wet in some rando."

"Well, you aren't getting it wet anywhere else, so I don't see why you'd shoot it down if the chick is even halfway hot," my idiot of a best friend states with a shrug as he turns his attention to the meager contents of my fridge. "Just saying, it's basically killing two birds with one stone plus the bonus of no awkward relationship talk while you're trying to find your boxers."

I knew I shouldn't have told him about my new job. Jeremiah's been on a mission to get me laid for the last eleven months ever since the night I showed up at his apartment, stumbling drunk, bleeding, and raging until I passed out cold on his kitchen floor.

"Whatever," is the only reply I can muster as I walk to the bathroom to wash the salt water off my skin before my "date."

It's impossible to be pissed, though. Jealous, sure, but not pissed. He's been my best friend for a decade and is living the life I once had, touring the world, and riding the best waves the universe has to offer. He's me a year ago but smarter because he had a front-row seat to my rise and a red-carpet invite to my downfall. He learned from my mistakes. All of them.

And not once has he treated me any differently.

He doesn't judge me when he hits the pocket spot-on and I flounder like a newbie. He has no pity when I bow out of a night of partying because my lousy budget is too tight. He picked his side the night I knocked on his door, howling my fury and heartbreak to the moon, and he's never wavered.

He just wants me to get laid.

With a towel wrapped around my waist, I acknowledge his exit with a wave and a promise to meet him at the beach at dawn, ignoring the box of leftover Chinese food tucked under his arm.

The guy may be raking in my old endorsement deals, but old habits die hard, and his friendship is worth more than an argument over two-day-old Kung Pao chicken. Besides, I have less than an hour to go from beach bum to black tie and get my broke ass into LA for a date I don't want with a woman I've never met for money I need to hold on to the last thing in my life that means anything.

****

Ryan

"Damn it, damn it, damn it, damn it."

Nothing gets my blood fired up quite like an avoidable inconvenience, be it a run in my last pair of comfortable nude stockings, losing my wireless earpiece, or wearing new shoes before breaking them in. Chanting my frustration may not solve my current problem, but it's helping to focus my annoyance and my breathing as I alternate between jogging awkwardly in these kitten heels and speed walking toward Maxwell's where Malcolm Sullivan is probably minutes away from jumping ship.

I never run late. Punctuality equals respect. Yet here I am, twelve minutes late, a light sheen of sweat on my forehead, my purse slapping against my hip with every step, and my boy shorts riding so far up my ass I'm tempted to unzip my jeans and yank them out.

That's right.

Jeans.

I'm running late toward the hottest restaurant in LA wearing distressed jeans, a yellow cardigan I knew was too bright for my pale complexion but bought anyway, and a black camisole with a scooped neckline threatening to dip under my boobs with every step.

I also have a wedgie.

I slow to a stop across the street from my destination, duck into a storefront, and check my makeup, knowing nothing can save me now.

Damn it.

Damn my hairdresser who does amazing work but

9

took an extra hour to tone down my caramel highlights. Damn my driver who's never late but left me waiting for thirty minutes while he changed a flat. And damn Renna for booking this black-tie date when she knew my roots were starting to show.

Damn it all.

Looking up from my compact mirror, I spot Malcolm leaning against Maxwell's brick exterior, filling out a sapphire-blue suit with the confidence of a man used to the appraising gazes raking over him. His jaw sports a faint stubble, and his blond hair is untamed, falling in loose waves with every comb-through of his fingers.

He's easily recognizable from the pared-down profile Renna sent my way last week. She knows I like going into these dates as blind as possible. I'm the final boss, the last gauntlet men must run before I'll sign off on their employment in my company. My anonymity is protected by my absence during the interviews, allowing me the freedom to test-drive the product before unleashing it upon my clients.

While my main priority is to watch for red flags, I also use the evening to study my future employee for weaknesses we can address in-house. Some need a crash course in black-tie expectations. Others benefit from a few one-on-one dance lessons. A few require more intensive conversation skill development, and the odd one needs manners coaching.

Any flaw we can repair, we do. The rest we market.

I pause a moment to assess our potential new hire. Doll Parts attracts its fair share of dark and dangerous, so blond and playful is definitely a nice change. Malcolm's photo collection included a shot of him playing frisbee, a selfie with a dog, and a candid taken at what looked like a bonfire, along with others showcasing a lean figure muscled through activity instead of honed at a gym.

Even from here, I see why Renna's side note referred to him as a colt posing as a stallion. The man is in constant motion. His broad shoulders roll. His hands alternate between the pockets of his fitted trousers and his hair. He tosses his head a fraction every so often. Yet somehow he manages to appear cool and composed, powerful with a hint of boredom, telling the world he's here until he no longer wants to be.

In a word, he looks unpredictable.

I, on the other hand, look like a hot mess. My fresh manicure is creased, my hair has gone from done to *done*, and I suspect the coffee stain my stylist swore I managed to blot out is visible. I'm seconds away from abandoning all professionalism and bolting.

But when Malcolm slides his phone from his pocket and checks it, the quickly schooled flash of concern on his face makes my decision for me.

I'm across the street before I can second-guess my decision, pulling up my mental first-date checklist to center myself as my carefully planned evening goes up in smoke.

"Malcolm?" I inquire, feigning the shy curiosity I channel with every initial meeting and ignoring the fact it's not feeling quite as fake as usual. "I'm Ryan. Ryan Rose."

Those empty blue eyes turn on me, and he freezes for a moment before his face breaks out in a warm smile. "It's great to meet you, Ryan. I was getting a little worried something happened to you."

I know instantly the slight rasp in his voice is going to be a hit with my clientele.

Had I not seen the concern for myself, I would have given him one bonus point for the expressed empathy. As it is, he gets two for being genuine. "My day got away on me." I hold out my arms, deciding to own my disastrous state as an excuse to reschedule for a night when I don't feel so unprepared and out of control. "Unfortunately, I'm nowhere near dressed appropriately for the evening I had planned."

"So we'll pivot," he replies with a grin as he undoes the top two buttons of his white shirt and shrugs off his jacket. He drapes it over his elbow and proceeds to roll up his sleeves, not-so-slyly checking me out while he does so. "There's a burger place two blocks over, and I know for a fact the dress code includes adorable chic."

Adorable chic.

Cute, and said with enough heat to make a woman feel pretty damn good in spite of her coffee-stained cardigan.

The urge to slow clap for him is strong, but it's nowhere near powerful enough to drown out my rising stress when I realize he's serious. "Pivot," I echo, not liking the taste of the word on my tongue. "But Maxwell's was the plan in my calendar. And you're all dressed up for it."

He bows his head and gives me a conspiratorial grin. "I'll let you in on a little secret, Ms. Rose. I hate wearing suits, so I'm going to grab on tight to any excuse to switch gears." Straightening, he offers his arm. "Shall we?"

Malcolm Sullivan receives another two check marks in the Manners column, but loses a dozen points in the

Puts Client at Ease column, because I'm anything but as I loop my arm in his and my fingers dig into his forearm.

I take a deep breath, regretting it the moment his scent hits me. The combination of a refined, woodsy cologne mixing with an undercurrent of a wild ocean breeze almost stops me in my tracks, and I stammer my weak protest. "Perhaps we should reschedule."

Rescheduling would be for the best. It would give me time to center myself, to regain control of the situation and start this test date anew on a day when I'm not off my game, when I'm not feeling unbalanced and easily distracted by something as silly as a man's skin warm under my touch.

"I suppose we could," he replies, his tone light while his leisurely stride leads us down a well-lit side street. "But it would be a shame to waste an evening as nice as this one by going our separate ways." His tongue runs along his full bottom lip. "Unless, of course, you had your heart set on an evening of dancing and fine dining, in which case I'd be honored to escort you to your car and reschedule for a later date."

He's graciously given me my out. All I need to do is call a cab, and I'll be free to return to my home, sink into a bubble bath, and scrub away all evidence of this frustrating day.

But when I open my mouth to thank him for being so accommodating, my new plan evaporates and something far too close to sincerity comes out. "I'm starving, I'm thirsty, and my feet hurt," I blurt, my eyes widening at the unbridled desperation in my voice. This test date has spiraled so far out of control before it's even started that I don't think there's any way to right the course. "I mean—"

"I hear you loud and clear," Malcolm says with a wink before he unhooks his arm from mine, drops to one knee, and offers his back. "Hop on."

Lord help me, I do.

Chapter Two

Malcolm

"I must be high," I hear Ryan whisper when I grasp her ankles, the death grip she has around my throat tightening a fraction as I rise up. "Hair-dye induced intoxication."

I would laugh if I could breathe.

The poor woman was nothing like the thoughts swirling through my head the longer I waited outside that stupid facade of a restaurant. It wasn't a place where the real movers in LA congregate. One look at the steady stream of influencers and self-proclaimed shakers walking in was proof of who the place catered to, and it was a crowd I knew well. It wreaked havoc on my nerves, the flashes of veneers and angles of selfies making me wonder what the hell I was doing pretending I could slip back into that lifestyle, even for a night.

But as the minutes ticked by, my anxiousness started to shift to worry.

After all, who spends hundreds of dollars on a guy, then stands him up?

I was moments away from calling the emergency number in Doll Parts to report a missing date when that gentle voice sliced through my souring thoughts and damn near knocked me on my ass.

Years of PR training was the only thing keeping me

from tripping over my own tongue and announcing the one thought barreling through my head in that instant.

Holy fuck, you're hot. Hot, hot, hot, hot—

I couldn't think of anything else to say to the gorgeous woman with large brown eyes so dark and intense I felt like I was looking into a bottomless pit I was more than ready to tumble into. Her cheeks were flushed, her lips stained red from lipstick that had long since worn away. Shoulder-length hair fell in soft, wind-blown waves, framing a heart-shaped face. One deep inhale and I was surrounded by a wild floral scent with a soothing hint of vanilla I wanted to bury my face in.

When I had the opportunity to check the rest of her out without detection, I had to fight the urge to stare. The neckline of her black tank top was off-kilter, revealing a hint of the lacy black bra beneath. Smooth, pale skin peeked out from the rips in her fitted jeans, and my mind instantly decided I wanted to run my tongue along each slit from her delicate ankles up to the promised land. Her sweater was a few sizes too large and almost swallowing her willowy frame, but it only added to the whole sweet and sexy thing she had going on.

Despite the cool demeanor she tried to project, I could tell she was flustered by the faint trembling of her fingers gripping her purse strap, and in that moment, I wanted nothing more than to put her at ease.

Too bad everything I did only seemed to make it worse.

Nothing about Ryan's casual appearance prepared me for the panic I saw in her eyes when I suggested we change our plans. Guilt hit hard, but when I offered to reschedule and all the tension in her body seemed to collapse in on itself with her admission she was hungry, thirsty, and sore, the good ol' hero complex I've been actively suppressing for the past year rose like a goddamn phoenix.

Glancing over my shoulder as I ease the stranglehold my passenger has around my neck, I give her a reassuring smile. "Comfortable?"

"No." She exhales then swallows hard. "But it's truly an 'it's not you, it's me' issue I'm having back here." She clears her throat delicately. "So your online profile mentioned you like to surf. Have you been doing it long?"

Her question snaps me back into my reality, reminding me the woman on my back is a job. "I grew up beside the ocean," I answer, being both truthful and vague. "Any oceanside kid who tells you he didn't surf—or at least try—is either lying or was embarrassingly bad at it."

She hums softly in my ear, and the slight ache in my knee flares as it does every time I talk about surfing with people who don't know who I used to be.

"How about you?" I press, knowing it's better to shift the topic of conversation to her than to leave an opening for her to delve too deeply into my own history. "Are you an LA native or a transplant?"

"Uprooted to Anaheim years ago and never left."

"So you're immune to fireworks and have innate distrust of talking mice?" I tease, lowering to my good knee as we reach our new destination.

She dismounts, and I feel the absence of her warmth immediately.

"Precisely." She laughs, her cheeks flushing when she looks down at the neckline of her tank top, which has gone even more astray. "I swear I'm not usually this much of a mess."

"I swear I'm usually much more of one," I counter, placing my hand on her lower back and escorting her inside.

The music of an unsigned band hoping to make it big pounds through cheap speakers, and the sound of chatter and utensils fills the crowded dining room. I take Ryan's hand and all but drag her to the only open table, pull her chair out for her, and get her seated before anyone else can stake their claim on the precious real estate.

Passing her one of the menus tucked between the napkin dispenser and the condiments, I steal a moment to watch her reaction to Jelly's Eatery, the best damn burger place in California and as far from the pretentiousness of Maxwell's as possible without risking salmonella.

Her dark eyes are taking in everything from the mash-up of street art on the walls to the twinkle lights strewn around the walls and windows haphazardly. People are jostling for space around the pinball machines, their vacated seats being guarded rabidly by those hanging back. Our own table is bumped as servers squeeze through with carefully balanced plates and trays. She inhales deeply, and I bite my lip, hoping I didn't make a mistake bringing her here.

"This is wild." She exhales, craning her neck to watch a skateboarder slip past us and wheel out the door with a takeout bag in his hand.

"We don't have to stay," I offer up, disappointed but not wanting her to feel obligated to not only be paying to spend time with me, but to spend time with me in a place she doesn't want to be.

A cheer swells up from the pinball game behind me, and Ryan gives me a smile bordering on giddy. "Are you kidding? I feel like if we leave now, I'll miss something super cool and I'll regret it the rest of my life."

****

Ryan

I've never been this full.

I've never laughed this much.

I've never had this much fun.

And I've never been as nervous about leaving a noisy, crowded restaurant as I am right now, because without a thousand stimuli assaulting my senses at once, I'm going to be left with only one, and he's dangerous as hell.

Malcolm refuses to let me pay for our dinner, claiming it's his way of making up for eating more than half of the chocolate tower cake we split after devouring our combined weights in burgers and fresh-cut fries. My sides are aching from two hours of easy conversation and laughter thanks to his ability to pull me out of my comfortable little shell. The mental checklists I use to guide these test dates were abandoned within minutes of our milkshakes arriving, and for the first time in years, I feel adrift.

I don't hate it, but I'm not liking it either. I'm off-balance and out of my element, unfamiliar with the looseness in my posture and the ease of my responses. We've kept our conversation light and superficial, yet I feel as though I know him. He's sweet and polite, funny without stooping to condescension or ridicule. We touched on everything from music to travel to books. We swapped embarrassing childhood stories and argued over whose fear was more debilitating while living in

Southern California—his trypophobia or my reptile-induced panic attacks.

What I figured would be a disaster of an evening has turned out to be one of the best nights I've had out in years.

Which is why I should end it now.

Malcolm takes my hand as we exit the mayhem of lights and smells and sounds and leads me back down the street, his giant mitt engulfing mine.

I should call my driver and head home since I have everything I need to give my final approval of Doll Parts's newest employee. He's passed with flying colors, and I don't need another hour or two to solidify my opinion. The man is a perfect addition to our catalogue, someone we can market toward first-timers who need someone to put them at ease. Judging from the last two hours, Malcolm can ensure even the most uptight woman has a memorable evening at his side.

We walk back toward Maxwell's in a companionable silence, and I can't suppress my disappointment that the date has come to an end.

Except instead of leading me toward the row of cabs waiting curbside, his hand tightens around mine and we dodge our way across the street before dropping onto a wrought iron bench.

"The blond guy with the blue streaks," he murmurs, nodding his head toward the front door of the restaurant where a man and his posse are striding in. "His tragic backstory includes three failed marriages by age twenty-nine due to his overbearing mother who he calls twice daily. He overcame his addiction to black licorice two years ago, but every day is a battle, and it sours the fame he's gained as a two-fingered blackjack dealer."

My manners evaporate as I stared slack-jawed at the guy across the street. "No way. Seriously?"

"Not a lick," Malcolm replies smoothly. "I just like making shit up about strangers."

My initial approval of him wavers. "What? Why?"

Shrugging, he grins, and I hate myself a little for the way my heart hiccups with that flash of dimple.

"Because it's harmless fun. Try it." His smile morphs into a solemn study of a group of diners walking into Maxwell's. "Those two with the matching haircuts. What's their story?"

I follow his gaze. "Um, they were double-booked at the salon, but neither would reschedule, so now they got matching cuts and colors to save time."

I can feel Malcolm's blue eyes searing into me as he sighs. "Everyone knows Lacey and Jacey are soul mates who met during a Brazilian-cruise leech-therapy session. Lacey popped the question four hours later, and they've been inseparable ever since despite never following through with the wedding because Jacey is saving up to marry in space."

When I respond with nothing more than an inelegant snort, he scoots closer to me and drapes one long arm across the back of the bench. "Now you try again."

And I do.

Heavens help me, I do.

I sit there with Malcolm Sullivan for the next hour, creating absurd tales about Maxwell's clientele, each story becoming more and more outlandish until I'm spending more time giggling than speaking.

Giggling.

In public.

While wearing a coffee-stained yellow cardigan.

"Okay," I finally say on an inhale as I fan the tears in my eyes. "Okay. Oh my." Taking a shaking breath, I try to regain my footing. "I hate to end this study into the human psyche, but I have an early meeting tomorrow, and I'm an absolute bear if I don't get enough sleep."

Earning another check in the Manners column, Malcolm stands and holds out his hand. "Can I give you a ride?"

As much as I want to hop in his truck and grasp on to another few minutes with him, the time for fun is over. "Thank you but no. I'll take a cab."

He doesn't rush us across the street this time. Instead, he offers his arm and leads me to a crosswalk half a block up, and I can't help but be pleased he's stalling the inevitable end of our time together.

When we arrive at the line of taxis, he opens the door for me, waiting until I'm seated and buckled before he speaks.

"Thanks for the great night, Ryan," he says, his gaze lingering on my lips for a moment before his eyes snap to mine. "I know it wasn't the date you wanted."

"Maybe not, but it was the date I needed."

The truth of my words hits me, and I swallow the bitter honesty as he lifts my hand to his lips and presses a gentle kiss on my wrist.

I don't need dates. I need the safety and security that comes with being in control of my life, my business, and my finances. I need access to my calendar and a reliable dry cleaner. I need detailed reports on my investments and properly fitted bras.

He closes the car door, taps the roof three times, then gives me a smile and a wave as the taxi pulls away.

The test date is over. He passed with flying colors.

I, on the other hand, failed miserably according to the rapid-fire of my pulse.

I skim my thumb along my wrist to clear away the thoughts that simple kiss conjures before I open Doll Parts app and, with the tap of a few buttons, end my night with Malcolm Sullivan.

Chapter Three

Malcolm

I have a real love-hate relationship with my phone.

I love ordering pizza while I coast the weak afternoon waves to shore.

I love texting Jeremiah to pick up a six-pack of beer on his way to my place because damn it, I deserve a cheat day.

I love opening up the Doll Parts app and seeing three more bookings this week.

I hate the real-time updates letting me know Ryan isn't one of them.

It's been twelve days since I saw her, since I watched her taxi drive off moments before my phone chimed with an app notification indicating our date was complete.

She gave me five stars across the board.

A two hundred dollar tip.

And then nothing.

Shaking the ocean water from my hair, I hike my board under my arm, sling my bag over my shoulder, and cross the hot sand toward my apartment.

I don't even know why it bothers me so much, why I've lain awake at night thinking about a woman who paid—*paid*—to spend time with me. Sure, she's gorgeous, and I've admittedly spent more than a few extra minutes in the shower jerking it to thoughts of her on her knees, those dark eyes looking up at me while her lips wrap around my cock.

Except this is California and gorgeous women are everywhere.

I couldn't describe Ryan as a showstopper with her coffee-stained yellow sweater. But a heart-stopper? Yeah, I'll gladly give her that title because I'm still trying to catch up those beats I missed when I first laid eyes on her.

It's not like I'm hard up for female attention. If anything, I still get a damn decent amount of it even without the endorsement deals or trophies. Chicks dig guys like me. They have these romanticized visions of long walks on the sand at sunset, bonfire parties, and hot days spent soaking up the sun and kissing in the surf.

They love the whole beach-bum idea until they realize the waves will always come first. Few are fans of five a.m. wake-ups to catch the best of the morning tide with the rest of the dawnies, and they sure as hell don't like finding sand literally everywhere. Women look at me and see a good time. A temporary time. When my face became plastered on ads selling everything from boards to swimwear to cologne, I gained a little more value, became a hunted commodity. For a blip in time, women looked at me and saw a future because I had one. A good one, I thought.

But times change, bodies fail, and life eventually provides a swift kick to the nuts, which leaves the body broken and thrashing at low tide.

"Cole, honey. Come here and settle an argument."

Detouring away from the stairs leading up to my place, I walk straight toward the woman calling me over.

"Hey, Emma. What did Wade do now?"

Her gray eyes twinkle with mischief, and I love to see it, knowing today is a rare day of energy for her.

"That husband of mine insists we need to do an Alaskan cruise once all these silly treatments are done, but I think we should tour Europe. The rest of the staff placed their vote, and since we're now in a deadlock, we need you to cast the deciding vote."

"Aw hell, you can't ask me to do that." I groan, running a hand through my wet hair. "If I say Europe, Wade will sell this place out from under my nose. If I say Alaska, you'll kick my ass."

"Of course I will, sweetie," she coos, reaching up to pinch my cheek with her brittle fingers. "Now choose."

I'm saved by Wade striding out the front door of Barreled, the surf shop he and Emma have owned since before I was born. It's the place I'm aiming to buy if I can come up with the money fast enough, the only place outside the ocean where I feel at home.

"Don't you even think of using those wiles of yours on the boy," Wade warns his wife as he smiles and bends to kiss the top of her head. The light in his eyes dims when a slight tremor goes through her thin body, but he hides it with the skill of a man who has been masking his worry for years. "About time you came by again, Cole. The regulars have been asking for you."

"Work's been busy," I reply, offering my hand to help Emma to her feet. "At the rate I'm going, I'll have no problem getting the downpayment for this place before the deadline."

Wade watches Emma hobble inside, his posture relaxing once she takes her position on the bright orange sofa at the back of the shop. "You know I hate putting this pressure on you, son," he murmurs, running his wrinkled hand over my board in appreciation. "Hell, I'd sign the place over to you today for a dollar if it wasn't for the medical bills."

My father introduced me to Wade and Emma before I could even walk, and from what Emma says, I took to them like I took to the water. Over the years, they became my cheerleaders, my confidants, and my conscience when that particular piece of myself was struggling. They gave me my first job and my first place to live, hosted my high school graduation party, and set me back up in the apartment above the shop when my life went to hell.

Buying Barreled is a dream I've held most of my life, one Wade and Emma encouraged and actively prepared me for. But when Emma's ovarian cancer came back four months ago and the treatment expenses hit, Wade had no choice but to give me an ultimatum.

"Don't think twice about it," I reassure him. "It's doing me good to have a goal right now, and the sooner I get my ducks in a row, the sooner you'll be off to Europe."

Scoffing, Wade inspects my board one more time before sending me away with a promise to come upstairs for a beer some night. We both know he won't, but as he did for me when I was growing up, he knows my door is open for him day or night.

I walk into the apartment I've called home for most of my teen years and adult life, then slide my board into place and hit the shower before Jeremiah or the pizza shows up. The hot water relieves some of the tightness in my knee but does little to shake the Ryan-induced tension knotting the muscles in my shoulders.

Maybe it was the kiss.

The Doll Parts rules on touch leave little room for interpretation. Lips on skin is a definite no-no, even if that skin is on the inside of a delicate wrist. Even if that skin is smooth and pale and smells like wildflowers.

The water starts to run cool as I mentally deconstruct every moment leading up to the one where I took her hand in mine and brought her wrist to my lips like one of those presumptuous assholes I used to play nice with at every industry party I attended.

But in my defense, when I realized she was actually leaving and the need to taste her rose fast and hard, I took the prudent option. My next choice was hauling her out of that taxi and dragging her to the bed of my truck so I could show her exactly what my mouth could do for her.

That had to be it.

I broke the rules and spooked her.

I wrap a towel around my hips, check Doll Parts one more time, and notice last night's date finally entered her rating, giving me five stars in everything except manners where a measly two now soils my perfect score.

Whatever.

I didn't sign up to play bodyguard-slash-mercenary for a woman hellbent on picking a fight with her ex-boyfriend and his new girlfriend. Getting her out of there while she was only slinging curses and drinks was as chivalrous as I was willing to be.

I head into my bedroom to dress, going with a pair of oversized cargo shorts and royal blue V-neck since I have no date scheduled this evening. Jeremiah arrives as I toss my towel in the hamper, two pizzas in one hand, a case of beer in the other, and my wallet between his teeth.

"Seriously?" I huff, snatching my wallet first and

throwing it on the counter to be decontaminated later.

He grins in response, making himself comfortable on my sofa and turning on the television. "Consider it payback for slobbering all over my board last week."

"You mean when your board bounced off my face because you goofed that aerial?"

"You still slobbered."

Running my tongue along the front teeth I'm grateful are still there, I join him and grab a slice.

Thirty minutes later, we've settled on a movie, both pizzas are gone, and my beer is warming in my hand. The buzzing of my cell yanks me out of my food coma, and I groan as I fight it out of my back pocket.

"Fucking fuck."

Jeremiah glances over. "Cara?"

Snorting, I nod and hit ignore on my ex-wife-slash-stepmom. "What gave it away?"

"The *fucking fuck* was a hint," my best friend replies, his light tone countering the heaviness of my own. "Why is she still calling?"

"The fuck if I know," I grumble, no longer caring about the movie flashing across the television screen because I know damn well why Cara calls. Why she never stopped, even while on her honeymoon paid for on my dime. But I won't be sharing that info with Jeremiah because I don't want the inevitable murder rap he'd get on my conscience. "Maybe she's broke and needs a few bucks to cover her next round of lip injections."

He mutters a few choice words but doesn't press it.

He knows better.

The calls continue every ten minutes for an hour, each one going unanswered until Cara finally gives up. My mood has steadily shifted from annoyed to frustrated to irritated with both her and myself. How I didn't see my ex for who she was before she waltzed off into the sunset with my heart, my money, and my pride is an unending source of self-flagellation around here. The signs were all there, but I was too starry-eyed and caught up in my seemingly perfect life to see them.

Cara was a walking twenty-one-year-old guy's wet dream. When her blue eyes met mine the night I signed my first endorsement, I was hooked. From her honey-blonde hair tumbling down her back to her D-cups paired with a tiny waist and smooth hips to those toned legs which went on forever, I was a goner out of the gate. She sidled up to me at the after-party, smelling like exotic spice and experience, her husky voice commanding me to hop in her convertible and go for a ride.

And what a ride it was.

Eleven years my senior, Cara spent our first nights together proving I knew nothing about sex. She knew how to handle every part of my body in a way I'd never experienced, taking control and pushing all the buttons I didn't know I had. Every encounter before her faded into a jumbled mess of fumbling inexperience as her expert hands and mouth took ownership of me, mind, body, and soul.

Though looking back without the rosy orgasm haze tinting everything, maybe not my mind or my soul. My dick, definitely. And that jackass inserted himself into every decision I made for the next three years.

Did I love her? In a way, yeah. I loved the idea of her. I loved the image we projected when we were arm in arm. I loved showing her off and seeing the jealous glares of every man in the room when we walked in.

And I loved the sex she wielded like a weapon.

Sometimes because she wielded it like a weapon.

We fought constantly, huge blowouts complete with door slamming, screaming, and waking the neighbors in the luxury condo I bought us three months into our relationship. The lows were bottomless pits of rage and frustration and pain, but the highs kept me coming back on the hunt for more. After another year of misery punctuated by brief interludes of ecstasy, I discovered the key to earning my way back between Cara's thighs was through a penance of sparkling gifts and weekend getaways. In return, she tossed me adoration and orgasms to feed my ego, just enough to keep me eager and hungry for more.

When necklaces and shopping sprees were no longer sufficient to atone for whatever I did wrong, I bought her a ring and tied my life—and my bank accounts—to hers.

The fighting stopped immediately.

Cara was happy. I was happy. My career was gold.

Was being the operative word.

My mood officially tanks as my thoughts continue to spiral and my knee begins to ache. Adjusting my position to relieve the pressure, I can't help but catch the flash of pity on Jeremiah's face before he schools his expression and doubles down on his interest in the action flick onscreen. The pizza in my gut sits heavily, the half-empty bottle of beer in my hand starting to look more appealing than it did twenty minutes ago.

Another buzz of my phone snaps me out of the funk I'm sinking into, and I glance down to see an alert from Doll Parts.

"It better not be one of your hot sugar mommas thinking she can wreck my plan to get shit-faced on your couch tonight," Jeremiah states, cracking open another beer and craning his neck to see my screen as I open the app. "My sister and her boyfriend are in town for two more days, and I can't do another night of pretending I don't hear what they're doing to my guest room."

Grunting, I shove him away. "No one's wrecking your plans, dumbass." I tap on my alerts, read the message, and close it up as I stand, biting the inside of my cheek to stop myself from grinning like an idiot. "Looks like I spoke too soon. I'm out of here. Chips are in the cupboard, don't open the door to strangers, and no girls allowed."

"You're ditching me for a chick?" Jeremiah gasps with feigned indignation, like he didn't do it to me last week.

"I'm ditching you for work. Big difference."

Technically, it's not a lie. I've had a request for a last-minute dinner date. So, work.

The fact Ryan made the request has nothing to do with the speed I accepted.

****

Ryan

"Two stars," I whisper as my driver pulls up to the busy Huntington boardwalk. "Two. Stars. Two stars."

Exiting the SUV with a thank-you, I smooth my retro blue plaid suspender dress over my hips and continue to chant the little fib I'll be telling Renna tomorrow when she questions why I'm out with Malcolm again.

Two stars for manners. Unacceptable for Doll Parts. Even if I happen to know the client who provided the rating has a habit of using our employees to get under her ex-husband's skin.

But two stars are two stars, and my job as CEO is to

ensure every man in our employ adheres to our high standards. Personally. Through coaching dates.

I have to stifle a groan as I mentally review my rationalizations, because Renna will never believe I altered my evening plans of hot yoga followed by a berry smoothie to drive thirty minutes for a casual date with one of our highest-rated employees because of a measly two-star review. I usually don't jump in until a series of lower ratings comes in, and the coaching is almost always done in-house and in my office. Booking and paying for any date with my own employees after the tester is unheard of.

Much like making a last-minute change to my calendar.

Exhaling a nervous breath, I lick my lips and square my shoulders.

I shouldn't be here.

Yet when I scan the busy sidewalk and see a grinning Malcolm sauntering toward me half a block up, I can't walk away.

He has a faint hitch to his confident swagger, but it doesn't detract from the vision of him in faded jeans and teal Henley that clings to every ridge of his muscled chest and arms. Everything from his damp, tousled hair to that slight bowleggedness that makes a woman think about what he's packing has my pulse ratcheting up. Knowing a sweet, fun guy is hidden beneath all the hotness is the reason I've been tracking his profile like a bloodhound, hunting for any reason to see him again.

I want one more shot to feel like I did twelve nights ago.

I want him to wreak havoc on my methodically controlled emotions again. I want to smile and laugh without watching the clock. I want to forget about investments and projections and market value for a few more hours.

And I want to do it with a man who knows nothing about me, who has no expectations and no ulterior motive. I want to see that genuine smile and hear his hoarse laugh. I want to relax and listen to his wild stories about strangers.

I want to not be me for one more night.

His blue eyes scan me from head to toe as he approaches, the warmth in them flaring with a dark heat. "You sure know how to make a man glad he hauled his ass off the sofa."

"Oh, um, thank you." I laugh nervously as my cheeks warm, leaving me borderline mortified.

I don't blush. Blushing shows weakness, and any weakness in the business world is exploitable. Over the years, I mastered the art of remaining calm, cool, and unaffected in the face of compliments, comments, and outright insults. Having seen even the most subtle of emotional reaction unravel a woman's reputation in a room full of sharks, perfecting stoicism early in my career was a must.

Malcolm's gaze heats as it pauses on my cheeks, and he bites his lip, motioning for me to spin.

And I do.

Heavens help me, I obey with a giggle. And while I hate myself a tiny bit for it, I can't help feeling lighter than I have since the last time I saw him.

"So where are we going?" he asks, linking his arm in mine.

My mind is blank.

Where *are* we going? When I saw those two stars

pop up, I snagged my chance to set up another date without thinking past the meetup point. Not once did I consider what we would do all evening, and the realization crashes over me like a bucket of ice water. I can feel my pulse skyrocket as I scan the storefronts for inspiration. Being unprepared is a nightmare for me, and I'm living it in front of a man hot enough to have his own underwear campaign.

I need control over my life like I need oxygen. Security and planning and schedules bring me more peace than any formulated meditative retreat I had no involvement creating ever could. Growing up in a hurricane of unpredictability thanks to my mother following her heart from one penniless leech to the next made me who I am today. Her hunt for her happily ever after drained her bank accounts as often as it drained her soul until both were empty enough to be swept up by any man who made good on the promise to whisk her away. Even if he was twenty years her senior, smelled like moldy apples, and whisked her away from our dated bungalow in small-town Iowa to an overgrown jungle acreage in Brazil when I was two months from graduating.

It's why I harbor no ill will for the woman who birthed me and raised me. She taught me to rely on no man, to put myself first and establish my own little empire. Her mistakes gave me the drive to work hard enough in high school to earn a full scholarship to the University of Southern California, and by the time she was on her way to South America, I was months from graduation and ready to stake my little piece of the corporate pie.

But now I have to make a decision without

examining all the available options, and I'm drawing a blank on words. "Um—"

He nudges me gently, pulling my attention from the myriads of neon signs glowing overhead. "Why don't we grab takeout at the cantina over there? I have all the fixings for a beach picnic in my truck."

And there it is, the rush of calm I felt the last time I was in Malcolm's presence. It floods my veins and seeps into my head, soothing the nerves and synapses that have been firing full steam ahead all week.

I'm at ease in a heartbeat, and my smile comes naturally. "Sounds like a plan."

The cantina is loud and bustling, much like the restaurant we went to on our first date. Malcolm navigates it fluidly, leading me to the counter. "What looks good?"

"Everything," I answer honestly, scouring the menu displayed behind the tills. "I can't decide."

And I can't. I haven't studied the menu beforehand, haven't selected my top three choices plus one backup. A string of meetings kept me from eating a half-decent lunch today, so my hunger is beginning to take control of my decisions.

"I know just the thing," he states, leaning forward to place his order with the server. "One appetizer sampler, one charcuterie board, one taco and one quesadilla sampler, and one of those dessert mash-ups."

He yanks his wallet out and pays before I can argue.

"I requested this date," I remind him, crossing my arms as I lean against the counter and giving him my best disciplinary glare. "The agreed-upon terms state I pay."

Shrugging, he braces his arms on either side of me and gives me a lopsided grin. "Consider this my way of trying to convince you to book me more frequently. You get free tacos. I get to see you in that dress. I count that as a win for both of us."

My mind is instantly flooded with visions of him caging other women against bar tops, and I can almost hear his sweet flirtations being whispered in their ears, making them feel like the most important women in the world.

Which is how it should be because he's a hired date. A hired date I employ.

And while that makes Malcolm very good for Doll Parts's bottom line, it doesn't bode well for whatever it is I'm trying to achieve by being here.

Chapter Four

Malcolm

The speed in which Ryan's defenses fly up would be impressive if I wasn't so damn eager to knock them down. Her whole body has stiffened, the enticing blush staining her cheeks when I met her outside replaced by the pallor I've noticed she gets when she's flustered.

I drop my arms, shove my hands in my pockets, and take a small step back to give her space, hoping like hell I didn't scare her when I moved in close and caged her against the counter to keep the jackasses behind us from knocking into her.

I pretend to track the order numbers flickering in red on a large screen behind the tills, grateful the music is loud enough to make conversation at this distance near impossible.

Our order number pops up, and I all but lunge toward the server holding out our food in a paper bag. "Right here," I announce, glancing over at Ryan and giving her a quick smile. "Ready?"

Her shoulders square as she takes a deep breath, and I brace myself for a firm but polite excuse to end this date before it begins.

Instead, she steps in tight to my side. "See the guy over there with the purple mohawk?"

Confused, I scour the dining room until I spot him.

"An ex?"

"No. He's an international spy who used to work for the Hungarian government, but he got mixed up with the underground Chula Vista punk scene, married a deadhead named Crystalline Snowdrops, and now teaches macrame out of his garage."

I grin. "Nice one."

Her small hand loops around my forearm, the other bracing against my bicep as I lead her out of the crowded restaurant and onto the busy sidewalk. I feel like a goddamn king as we walk in companionable silence to my truck where I grab the blankets and water bottles I keep stashed in the cab.

Within minutes we're sitting on the sand in the early evening sun, a virtual feast before us.

"Oh God." She moans, biting into a quesadilla. "This is good. So, so good, Malcolm."

My dick responds to the sound of my name on her lips, and I tear into a taco to give my brain a chance to take back control.

It doesn't happen for a while.

Ryan is practically orgasmic over the meal. She gasps and groans. Her eyelashes flutter. Her lips purse. Her tongue swipes.

I feel like a Peeping Tom watching her eat, like she's putting on my own private show if I pretend every asshole who walks by isn't thinking exactly what I am every time she licks salsa off her fingers.

By the time she pushes the dessert tray away with a satisfied sigh, I'm as hard as stone and ravenous for a lot more than flatbread.

"That was incredible," she says with a sheepish smile as she eyes the empty platters. "I probably shouldn't work through lunch if I want to make a good impression on a dinner date."

Making sure my shirt conceals the effects her food porn had on me, I recline onto my back and tuck my hands under my head so I don't give in to the urge to bury them in her hair. "I'd say not abandoning me to eat all that on my own while you pick at a leaf makes a damn good impression."

She mimics my position and laughs. "I'll add 'participates heartily in meals' to my client profile when I get home."

Taking the opening, I go for the question that has been burning a hole in my head for twelve days. "Can I ask why you even have a client profile? You're gorgeous and sweet and don't give off any red-flag-crazy vibes. I mean, of all the dates I've been on through Doll Parts, you confuse me the most."

Her dark eyes widen before she looks away and studies the sky. "I, um, work a lot."

"What do you do?"

She pauses. "I'm a director of human resources."

I wait for more, but she doesn't elaborate.

And I get it.

I'm a date for hire. There's a unique level of anonymity in a situation like ours because neither of us are expected to share anything personal. With the rest of my clients, I like the barrier, even if some of them breach it with intimate details I definitely don't need to hear. But with Ryan, I want to know where she works and whether she likes her boss. I want to know if she suspects her coworker is eating the yogurt out of her lunch and what she really thinks about the new hires.

"So you work too much to date?" I press, fishing for

any information I can about her relationship history without outright asking.

She takes a deep breath and rolls onto her side to face me. "That's part of it."

"And the other part?"

Her brows furrow, and she bites her lip. "I like the structure of this," she finally says. "There are clear rules and expectations and boundaries. Everything is laid out ahead of time, the guys are vetted thoroughly, there's a definitive start and end, and I have control over the when and where. I, um, don't do well with unpredictable."

Guilt hits me. "Shit, Ryan, I'm sorry. This is twice I've just kind of taken control over where we were going and what we were doing." I run a hand over my face with a groan and stretch out on my back. "I swear I'm not usually this much of a bulldozer."

She's quiet for a moment, and I'm afraid to look over until I feel her fingers wrap loosely around my pinkie. "I don't mind your kind of unpredictable."

****

Ryan

Two stars.

I'm supposed to be working, supposed to be guiding Malcolm to ensure his ratings are top-notch. Quality is the cornerstone of Doll Parts, and it's my job to maintain the standards I set for this company the day I started it.

But for the life of me, those two stars have taken a backseat to lying side by side with him on a blanket, watching the sun set over the ocean.

"Can I ask you a question?" I say softly.

"Fire away. For you, I'm an open book."

Somehow I believe him. Maybe I simply want to think our "dates" are different than all the others he's paid to go on, but the sincerity in his voice gives me a strange sense of hope. "You said out of all your dates, I'm the one who confuses you…" I venture, leaving the statement hanging because I know I'm treading on dangerous territory professionally.

"Well, yeah." He shades his eyes and looks over at me with a grin. "Confidentiality says I can't say much, but I'll say this—Doll Parts told me I would have a variety of clients, but so far I've had nothing but older rich women who view me as a toy or a show dog. They want a guy on their arm so they aren't alone while they hunt for their next meal ticket. And then there's you."

I can't miss the disdain in his voice with the words older rich women, and I wince internally as I do a mental review of his clients so far and realize I am precisely who he means.

It also means we haven't marketed him to the full spectrum of our client base, an oversight I'll need to rectify in the morning.

"It doesn't bother me or anything," he adds, his nose wrinkling. "It is what it is, and I signed up for it willingly. They just aren't the kind of women I would ever spend my downtime with."

Although I know I'm wading deeper into dangerous waters, I continue to press. "What kind of women do you spend your downtime with?"

He swallows and reclines back, tossing an arm over his eyes. "I don't."

Oh.

Oh.

I don't know why it never occurred to me, and I wince, my mind immediately scouring every moment we've spent together for the clues I missed. "I shouldn't have assumed," I say by way of apology. "What kind of guys do you spend your downtime with?"

There's a solid thirty seconds where he goes completely still, and I feel even worse for barraging him with questions I have no business asking.

I'm usually better than this. I've made a career out of reading people and situations, assessing their wants and needs and adapting to their personalities to avoid conflict. Prying is a cardinal sin. While some tight-lipped people will open up under the right conditions, they tend to raise their guards even higher afterward, all trust erased as they protect their exposed bellies.

Malcolm sits up and drapes his long arms over his knees as he studies me. "You're totally freaking out right now, aren't you?"

"No," I scoff, copying his pose while paying careful attention to the hang of my skirt. "Of course not. I didn't say anything."

He smirks. *Smirks.* "You didn't have to. You've gone pale, you're biting your lip like it's your last meal, and I think you've blinked a hundred times in the last minute."

Taking a deep breath, I glower at him, refusing to blink even once. "I am not."

I suddenly feel as though I'm back in grade school and my crush—Jimmy McCutcheon for three years, to be precise—is teasing me about liking him.

"You are. It's cute. And no, guys aren't my thing. I just have a lot going on right now, and a girlfriend fits into exactly none of it." Malcolm bumps his shoulder against mine gently. "Though if I did have a type, I think it would be pretty human resource directors with brown eyes and blue dresses."

I find my balance immediately.

This I know. It's in my wheelhouse, this casual textbook flirtation. I not only encounter it while networking, but I also coach our employees on how to use it without sounding sleazy, slimy, skeezy, or a combination of all three.

"Aren't you a charmer?" I say with a smile as he stands and offers his hand to help me to my feet. "So what now?"

He gathers up the blankets, shakes out the sand, and slings them over his shoulder while I collect what's left of our picnic. "First, we drop these back at my truck. Then we're walking to the pier."

He takes my hand in his like it's the most natural thing in the world, and off we go.

Chapter Five

Ryan

The first step to recovery is admitting you have a problem.

Staring at my reflection in my private office washroom, I confess my weakness to myself.

I'm a stalker.

The disclosure does nothing to remove the weight of guilt or the stench of deception.

On the other side of the door is my computer, eighteen different tabs and programs open. Sixteen of them are a mix of spreadsheets, calendars, resumes, and financial records.

One is Malcolm Sullivan's profile, listing his age as eleven years younger than me and noting his allergy to mold.

Except the mold isn't what I'm zooming in on.

No, that would be his profile picture zoomed in on that damn dimple in his right cheek.

The last tab is his schedule. His fully-booked-with-a-waiting-list schedule.

It's been two weeks since we walked along the beach and out to the pier where we sat side by side on the weathered wooden boards, our feet dangling above the water. He told me about his mom who walked out on him and his dad when he was three. I told him about growing up with a single mother who loved the idea of love more than she understood it. Financially, his upbringing sounded more stable than mine, but although my mom moved us from the home of one man to the next in search of her happily ever after, I knew she loved me in her own way.

From the little Malcolm spoke of his father, I don't think he could say the same.

Straightening my spine, I step back from the mirror and smooth my green silk blouse, tucking it tighter into my black pencil skirt. The shine of the emerald stone hanging from the thin gold chain around my neck catches my eye, and I blow out a puff of air.

Director of human resources, my ass.

If Malcolm saw me now, dressed in my red-soled heels and slipping on a tailored suit jacket in my private en suite, the playful openness I've become obsessed with would evaporate in a blink.

Every review he's received in the last two weeks has been glowing. Those assessments combined with the front-page feature on our website have made him Doll Parts's hottest commodity among our clients searching for a man to make them look good. Malcolm is the perfect date for parties, dinners, soirees, and social gatherings. He's attentive and well-spoken, polite and professional. Accolades are given for his discretion and his ability to blend in with producers and CEOs and high-priced lawyers. The few clients he's accompanied into the ocean for boogie-board lessons have raved about his patience.

And he looks positively bitable in a suit, be it tailored or swim.

But not a single comment mentions his sense of

humor or how smoothly he puts his clients at ease. There isn't one remark about how his smile is downright contagious or how far down the rabbit hole he can go on topics he's interested in.

For the record, javelinas are one of those topics. He has an impressive—if not a little peculiar—amount of knowledge about those little not-pigs.

With a final glance in the mirror, I step back into the real world where my phone is buzzing incessantly on my desk and Renna is leaning against the wall examining her yellow nail polish.

"We need to talk about the new recruit," she states without looking away from her long fingers. "The yearling."

Frowning as I cross the room, I slide into my chair and pull up my master list of employees before making the connection. "You mean Malcolm Sullivan."

"Do you know any other excitable baby stallions galloping around here?"

I freeze. "Here? As in right now?"

"As in he's sitting in the reception room and probably bouncing off the walls waiting for an answer."

I fix my gaze on my computer screen and attempt to read over the monthly expense report while I panic internally.

He's here. In my building. In my reception room.

There's no escape.

If he sees me, he'll know I lied about my job and who I am. He'll know Ryan Rose—his slightly neurotic date and inhaler of tacos—is Adrian Dawson, CEO of Doll Parts and his boss.

It shouldn't matter, because I have no intention of booking another date with him. Renna's radar aside, I've already pushed my luck in crossing the professional lines I drew in permanent marker the day I opened shop.

But he's here. And he wants an answer—

"What's the question?" I finally ask, feigning exasperation at having to deal with anything outside of my perfectly crafted schedule.

Renna crosses her arms. "He wants to open his schedule to twenty-four hours, seven days a week."

Frowning, I glance over her shoulder at the closed door, like I might be able to see through the heavy wood if I try hard enough. "Reason?"

"He won't say." My best friend pushes off the wall and approaches my desk. She splays her hands across the top as she leans in. "My gut tells me he has money problems. Big ones. Big enough to make him a potential liability if he starts accepting money for—" Her lip curls in disgust. "For other services."

Oh God.

My imagination splinters off and slams against the ceiling, projecting an image of Malcolm and last night's client fucking like rabbits in an upscale hotel room. I haven't seen him naked, but my brain has no trouble filling in the missing pieces. I know it's him from the movement of his muscles rippling across his back and the sun-kissed highlights in his long hair.

I can't think. Or move. Or spe—

"You need to claw it out of him."

My attention snaps to Renna as she straightens up and crosses her arms over her chest. "What?"

"Claw it out of him," she repeats. "I'll add a few select openings to his schedule that happen to sync up with your availability, and I'll slide you in. We'll pay for it out of the training expense account since, technically, teaching that boy his dick isn't for sale as long as he's employed here is educational."

I know I need to respond, but I don't trust my voice.

And it scares the hell out of me.

I can command a room filled with the suavest of Los Angeles's elite. Compartmentalizing is my super power. Control is my middle name.

But apparently, all Malcolm has to do is exist somewhere on this planet to send me into a tailspin.

He's my damn kryptonite.

Renna stares me down. Her hands move to her hips. "It's the best way to find out if he's going to do anything to jeopardize the integrity of Doll Parts," she continues. "He referred to 'Mr. Adrian Dawson' when he made his request, so no one has tipped him off about who you are. We can use that and plan dates where there's no chance of running into anyone who can out you before we have an answer."

Drumming my fingers on the rosewood desktop to hide the slight tremble in my hands, I pretend I'm not becoming giddy over the prospect of best-friend-sanctioned dates with Malcolm. "You don't usually take risks like this. Surely, the income he brings in doesn't counter the potential losses or legal nightmare. Why not release him from his contract like you do the others you suspect of using their position here for unsanctioned financial gain?"

A low growl rumbles out of Renna. "Because he's cute, okay? He's like this overeager mastiff puppy who has no clue how big he is and just wants to play. I want to pick him up and take him home and let Brit feed him from the table. I don't want desperation to ruin him."

The visual has me laughing, imagining Renna's wife

scratching Malcolm under the ear and cursing his name as he jumps on the sofa. "You're a strange woman, Ren. But you're right. Play off the extra openings as a compromise Adrian Dawson is willing to make for the time being."

With her face still twisted up from exposing the nurturing side she usually camouflages through indifference and sarcasm, Renna nods. "I'll get right on it. Oh, and make sure you invest in a new bathing suit or two."

"Why?"

The evil smile replacing her discomfort is almost terrifying. "In the spirit of disarming him and putting him at ease on his home turf, the yearling is going to teach you how to surf."

****

Malcolm

My dad is a dick.

Not a regular dick either. A massive dick. An absolute dick. A dick of epic proportions.

Acknowledging it doesn't do anything for my state of mind, but chanting the words are helping with my board-waxing rhythm.

The freshly painted orange letters of Barreled's sign stand out like a warning against the white background, reminding me how far my father will go to fuck me over.

Emma and Wade retreated inside after they delivered the news of Billy Sullivan's interest in buying their shop, the fire in Emma's apologetic eyes letting me know they felt as bad about the situation as I was feeling. Wade's colorful language echoed my own thoughts, his frustration over being backed into a corner coming through in his aggressive reorganizing of the board display out front.

And they don't even know the half of it.

I don't blame them one bit for putting the buyout on a blind bid. A lifetime of hard work and sun shows in the lines of their faces and the wrinkles on their hands. They deserve a retirement free from the financial stressors Emma's illness brought.

The fact they're holding tight to their deadline to give me a fighting chance speaks volumes and helps smooth the jagged attack of their announcement. And I know if things were different and they were given the choice between me and the man they stepped up to replace in my life, they'd choose me every time.

But that isn't reality. Not mine, at least.

No, my reality includes my asshole of a father staking claim on my life again.

With a fresh topcoat of wax applied to one of my spare boards and the sand hot under my feet, I shake off the doom-and-gloom cloud hanging over my head and focus on the only good thing to come out of the mess I'm in—Ryan.

I'd all but begged the bright peacock of a secretary at Doll Parts to forgo the forty-hour-per-week availability requirement and allow me to open my schedule up completely. Hell, I'd even asked her to talk to the owner of the company, some Adrian Dawson guy I'd yet to meet.

When she informed me the best she could do was give me three extra blocks a week, I had no choice but to accept it even if it was a far cry from what I wanted. I left the office frustrated and beaten down, my mood sour and borderline explosive. But when my phone chimed minutes later with notifications letting me know I had new bookings and I saw Ryan's name, I damn near ran back up those stairs and kissed the peacock on top of her turquoise head.

The last two days dragged as I waited for our date this afternoon. I helped Wade out in the shop, hit the morning waves, joined Jeremiah on the water during one of his training sessions, went to two gallery openings, and catalogued the board collection in my spare room until I decided on the perfect one for Ryan's surf lesson.

Late afternoon on a weekday is a slower time on the water. Families pack up and go home with cranky toddlers, night-owl workers abandon the beach to prepare for work, and the evening crew is a good two hours from hitting the waves. It's a perfect time to teach a beginner to surf.

While the weight of my father's interference in my life is still hanging around my neck, I can't deny the excitement lightening my steps as four o'clock approaches. I admit I'm a little baffled why a woman like her is paying through the nose to hang out with a guy like me, but this is one gift horse I have no interest in unveiling because being with her makes me feel good.

I haven't felt good in a long time.

Scanning my supplies one last time, I second-guess the promo board I chose. Safety-wise, it's a solid choice on paper. But I received it after my injury and never tested it myself.

I should test it.

Except time's up, because a stunning brunette in a long-sleeved black wetsuit and gray board shorts hanging low on her hips is walking my way and I have a jaw to lift from the sand.

"Beach baby!" I call out as Ryan makes her way

toward me. "Ready to make the ocean your bitch?"

"Ready to humiliate myself in front of all these fine people, yes," she says with a laugh, her cheeks turning that enticing pink shade my dick has become Pavlov's dog over. She sets a lime-green bag on the blanket I put out for us and looks at me expectantly. "In case I wasn't clear in my booking info, I have zero skill."

I fight the urge to wrap my arms around her and pull that tight little body flush with mine, but it isn't easy. My head understands this isn't a real date and I can't afford to do anything to risk a job which pays this well. My body isn't quite comprehending why it can't scoop this gorgeous woman up and bury my face between her thighs.

Easing her board down to the sand, I do the one thing I know she's okay with—I take her hand. "You don't need skill as long as I'm here to coach you." Her fingers lace with mine, and her nails graze my skin, sending a shiver through me while I blatantly check her out. "And if this lesson is a bust, at least you can honestly say you're the hottest non-surfer surfer chick on the coast."

She bites her lip and looks up at me with those warm, flirtatious brown eyes. "You've got this sweet-talker thing down to an art, don't you?"

"What can I say? You inspire it."

She laughs, and I grin down at her, knowing I sound cheesy as hell but not giving a damn.

"Okay, coach. Show me how to own those waves."

Chapter Six

Ryan

Renna has been my best friend for so long I don't remember life without her.

But I'm going to learn what it's like soon, because I'm going to kill her. At least, I will if I don't die in the ocean first.

Another wave threatens to knock me off-balance, and the board tethered to my ankle bumps my arm. Strong hands grip my waist to steady me, and Malcolm's voice is low in my ear.

"I got you. Ready to try that pop-up again?"

No. No, I am not. If the choice is get on that demon board or stand here with a wall of solid muscle pressed up against my back, I'm going with the muscle.

But I don't say that, because I'm here to learn, and damn it, I'm going to learn.

"Okay," I grind out as he steps aside, and I grip the board, gracelessly mounting it and lying flat on my stomach. "Tell me again what's wrong with belly-boarding?"

"It's not surfing," is the only reply I receive.

I look over my shoulder to glare at him, my eyes narrowing when he gives me a dimpled grin.

"Watch the wave, baby, not me."

My internal dialogue has been little more than a

string of curses since we left the safe, sturdy beach and paddled out into the water.

Though technically, I paddled. Malcolm waded along at my side and checked out my ass more than was probably appropriate for a surf coach. Not that I was complaining about it because I was too busy complaining about things that mattered. Like my impending death.

"Here it comes," he calls out behind me. "Pop that ass up!"

I spot the wave he wants me to ride, and I'm on my feet moments later. The water lifts my board with me on it. It's the second time out of dozens that I've nailed my position, and I can feel the difference from my failed attempts as I ride the wave all the way to the shore, Malcolm's hollered encouragement in my wake. I hop off the board before I eat sand, scoop it under my arm, and turn to see him standing in the surf beckoning me back.

So I go.

My body is aching, I have sand in my hair, and my expensive waterproof mascara lied, but I go because there's a guy with the patience of a saint waiting for me.

The smile greeting me when I finally paddle close to him isn't the pleased, proud one I saw when I landed the wave. This one has me thinking about the sharks swimming nearby, the ones I'm certain are aching to sink their teeth into my thighs the moment they have the chance.

"You did it," he says, grasping the nose of my board and leading me deeper into the ocean where I know scientists have yet to venture. "Now we're going to try something else. Scoot forward and crouch down on your knees."

We're still moving away from shore, and I'm beginning to wonder what I know about this man and his surfing skills. Sure, he's probably better than me, but I haven't even seen him on a board. I have zero proof he knows what he's doing out here. For all I know, he could be a serial killer Renna conspired with to take me out because I made her attend that conference in Oklahoma three years ago.

Malcolm seems oblivious to my internal panic as he dives down, appearing behind me moments later. "Hold on," he warns. "I'm getting on."

"What do you mean 'getting on'?" I shriek. "There's no room! You've seen the movie. I know you have. There's not enough room, Jack. We'll tip or sink and then drown." I whimper and grip the board tight as it jostles beneath me. "We're going to die, aren't we?"

"Maybe. But we'll have a blast on the way. And for the record, there was more than enough room on that raft, Rose."

He's laughing. Not really, but I can hear it in his voice, in the low rasp in my ear. Glancing over my shoulder to see him paddling us farther out, I fix him with the stare I've used to make grown men shake in their tailored woolen trousers. "I'm giving you one star."

"And I'm giving you thirty seconds to ready yourself for your pop-up," he replies as though I haven't threatened him with everything I have. The board turns toward shore and stills in the quiet before a cresting wave. "Your whole job is to balance. I'll do the rest."

"The rest of what?"

His command to pop up comes fast, and I obey without hesitation, planting my feet as the biggest wave I've tackled so far carries us. Malcolm's shadow rises behind me, the board angles to the right a fraction, and I realize he's controlling our movement along the water.

One large hand engulfs mine, and I risk looking back, my balance wobbling enough to make me crouch lower to the board.

Malcolm's expression is a mixture of determination, concentration, and pure joy as he steers the board with skill and confidence. I can feel the shift in the hard plastic beneath my feet while we ride the wave, the motions fluid and controlled. I don't notice I'm smiling so wide my cheeks are aching as much as my glutes until we close in on the shallow water and he releases my hand.

"That was incredible!" I squeal, dropping to my knees when he dismounts with the grace of a panther. "Oh my God, Malcolm! Did you see how big that wave was? We didn't die!"

He's already turning the board back to the surf and guiding it forward while I ramble on and on about the rush, the thrill, and all the feels I just experienced. We ride the waves in three more times—Malcolm leading us farther and farther out each time—before I have to admit I can't physically handle another one.

Mentally, however, I could spend the rest of my life doing this.

It's an incredible sensation, coasting on the water with nothing else to think about except the subtle changes in the wave's motion and the man commanding the board behind me. I'm exhausted and sore as we hit the sand the final time, but I feel light. Relaxed. Alive.

"Looking a little unsteady out there, Cole," an older man calls out while he steps onto the beach. "You want me to open a space in my Saturday crew for you?"

Malcolm gets down on one knee to undo my board

leash and chuckles. "Sure. I'll show those six-year-olds what a real surfer can do while you're out there floundering in the pocket."

The guy gives us a lopsided smile as he passes. "Seriously, kid, you looked damn good out there. Even with a newbie on the board."

"He made me look good," I chime in, still riding the high despite my calf muscles screaming at me.

"Honey, you make you look good," the man growls, laughing uproariously when Malcolm stands and knocks him in the shoulder. "Okay, okay. I'm out. You two have a great rest of your evening."

Malcolm turns to me, scooping the board under his arm, slinging his gear bag over his shoulder, and sliding his phone out of the side pocket. "Aw hell. I didn't realize I kept you out there so long. How are you holding up?"

"I think dying is next on my agenda," I answer, only half-kidding while I text my driver my exact location to save as many steps as possible. "But since I have back-to-back meetings all day tomorrow, curling up on my bed and groaning until my alarm goes off in the morning will have to suffice."

He gives me one of those lopsided smiles that warms my insides and makes me think unchaste thoughts. "I really wish we had more time. I make a mean spaghetti and give wicked G-rated rubdowns."

I know better than to suggest we add another hour or three to our date because his timetable is imprinted in my memory.

He's scheduled to play arm candy at a film premiere with one of our most dedicated clients. It's his second booking with her, so I know he must have made a strong impression on her last week when she requested his presence at an art showing.

Financially, I'm pleased he made it onto her repeat list. It's good for both him and Doll Parts.

Personally, I want to punch sand.

He detours to a surf shop across the way and slides his board among the others on display before taking my hand and letting me lead him to the corner where my car service is pulling up. His voice drops to a whisper as he leans in close to my ear. "Your driver used to run a multimillion-dollar vegan-friendly restaurant chain before he was caught swallowing live minnows in the back of a steakhouse. His wife left him for his aura reader, but he found his soul mate a month later at the ER while waiting to have his hand removed from his French horn."

I laugh at the absurdity despite my surprising unwillingness to walk away from him.

He gives my fingers a squeeze. "I'll see you Friday, same time, same place?"

The hopefulness in his voice eases some of the jealousy I feel knowing where he's going next. "I'll be here, ready to show you how a real wave gets ridden."

His gaze drops to my lips and lingers. "I look forward to getting my ass kicked."

We stay in an odd standoff for a moment, me wondering if he'll cross the line and him staring at my mouth like he wants to not only cross the line but obliterate it with a healthy dose of TNT.

Then, exhaling long and hard, he backs up a step. "See you Friday, Ryan."

I'm almost crawling through my penthouse toward my bed, every muscle in my legs tight and cramping, when I remember the date had a purpose.

****

Malcolm

Kaliah is a fun date. Old enough to be my mother, she introduces me as her son's friend's cousin twice removed while we move among the Hollywood crowd filling the small theater. She knows everything about everyone, whispering devious—yet lighthearted and only mildly embarrassing—stories she knows about each person we encounter.

She treats me like a buddy, someone to tell borderline inappropriate jokes to between speeches. Her laughter is loud and full, her energy boundless as we head into the fifth hour of wine and appetizers and compliments on her directing skills.

I'm surrounded by up-and-coming actresses, the floor packed with gorgeous women in expensive dresses revealing thighs and cleavage and a whole lot of side-boob.

And my fingers are itching to open the Doll Parts app and message Ryan.

Just to check in with a quick *hey, how are you holding up?*

I can't shake the sight of her popping up on the board, her dark eyes narrowed in concentration and her expression one of fierce determination. Her board shorts and wetsuit didn't flash an inch of skin below her knees, yet simply thinking about her rising out of the water after she biffed it has me hard.

"Amarie came on the market two weeks ago," Kaliah murmurs in my ear, nodding to a waifish blonde checking me out with the lazy appreciation of a woman who knows what she wants. "Rumor is she's waiting for her ghost lover to propose, but is playing the field until he makes his move."

When my only response is to lift a brow, she chuckles. "Okay, okay. I'm done trying to play matchmaker for you. It's obvious you have someone on your mind and no woman here can sway you."

I refuse to confirm her suspicion, but it doesn't matter. Twenty minutes later, she sends me home with a kiss on the cheek, an impressive tip, and a veiled threat of making me spill the beans about my secret crush on our next outing.

I'm showered and in bed by midnight, my phone in hand while I debate messaging Ryan on the Doll Parts app.

As long as I focus on our surf date coming up, I can probably get away with it. But we already confirmed the place, date, time, and activity. Nothing can mask what I'm doing here—shooting my shot with a woman I'm contractually obligated not to pursue.

I open the app and tap on the messaging icon, my thumb hovering over her name way too long before I decide to go for it.

—*It's been a long time since I had that much fun on the water. Thanks for braving the waves with me.*—

It's nearly one a.m., so I slide my phone onto my night table and flop onto my back, not expecting an answer until morning. If at all.

Five minutes later my cell chimes.

—*It's been a long time since I've had that much fun, period. Thanks for dragging me along.*—

—*What are you doing up?*—

—*Cursing your name every time I move. You?*—

—*Just got home from a date.*—

The moment I send those words, I'm hit with a wave of guilt.

She knows what my job is and what the constraints are, but it feels like I'm cheating on her. And I have no idea how to deal with it.

—*Can I be real honest here?*—

—*Go for it.*—

—*I spent the whole evening working up the nerve to message you.*—

—*Funny. I did the same. Looks like you're braver than me, though.*—

What the fuck?

I'm sitting in the dark, grinning like a fool because this woman admitted she thought about messaging me. Not kissing me, not fucking me. Messaging me. And it's like I'm thirteen again and Jamie McAllister just told me Shawna Cain has a crush on me.

—*Think we could maybe continue this conversation off the app tomorrow? I know you're busy as hell all day, and I don't want you falling asleep mid-meeting.*—

I have a long wait before she messages me back, but when she does, she answers with a phone number, and her little icon goes dark letting me know she's gone offline.

My grin morphs from a dopey giddiness to pure satisfaction.

I got her number, and shit just got a hell of a lot more fun.

And complicated.

Chapter Seven

Ryan

My mother once told me I was more like her than I wanted to admit. She was on her seventh fiancé the night she sat my sixteen-year-old self down to tell me we'd be moving again, this time into a condo four hours from my high school.

"You're just like me, Adrian Rose. When you jump in, you do it with both feet," she said, her attempt to soften the uprooting of my teenage life falling flat as she tried to liken her impulsiveness to my single-minded drive to escape the merry-go-round of men and homes she kept us on throughout my childhood. "You're determined to win at life. I'm determined to experience it. And we both rationalize the choices we make to ensure we win our game."

An hour ago, I could still say she was wrong.

An hour ago, I could continue to overlook the decisions I'd made and the toes I crunched while I eked out my place in the business world, because the one thing I didn't abandon on my rise was loyalty. My word was credible, my reputation stoic but fair. Renna and Brit trusted my instincts and my judgment, and they stood at my side from the start when all I had to offer them were low wages, scratched desktops, and outdated computers.

But an hour ago, I didn't have tracks to cover.

Using my admin privileges and limited tech knowledge, I delete the last of the messages Malcolm and I exchanged and hope to hell I've covered my tracks enough to avoid Brit's detection.

I log out, close my laptop, and stare at my ceiling, knowing sleep won't come easy in the five hours I have before my day begins again.

Guilt weighs my thoughts. Guilt over lying to Malcolm, guilt over concealing my actions from the two women who've had my back from the beginning, and guilt over breaking my own ethics code.

And for what?

A man.

I want to scream into the darkness, but I can't find the energy to do it. Or the will. Because if I'm being honest with myself—and since I'm the last one I'm being honest with anyway—I have no regrets.

Malcolm feeds something inside me I didn't realize was starving beneath my lists and meetings and color-coordinated calendar entries. He makes me want to be in the moment instead of looking to the future. His calm unwinds the knots in my shoulders better than the hot yoga class I signed up for every Thursday but skip twice a month because something has to give. And what gives first is whatever isn't paramount to success.

Plus, he's hot.

Heaven help me, the man is hot, hot, hot, and I can't not think of those muscled forearms and strong hands and blue eyes. My concentration has gone to hell. Every flash of blond has me thinking about the almost imperceptible head toss he does whenever his hair falls across his forehead. The scent of saltwater and a crisp ocean breeze makes my pulse race. I zone out to thoughts of his lips and tongue and what they could do to me, all while I'm supposed to be running numbers and schmoozing investors. I'm lying awake thinking about him when I know I need to be in top form while I review my stock portfolio in the morning.

Malcolm's presence in my life is doing my career no favors.

But my financials and reputation are sound enough to weather this temporary insanity, so with the resolute decision to enjoy it while it lasts, I roll over and pretend to sleep until my alarm goes off.

****

Malcolm

Texting with Ryan is far more entertaining for me than she realizes.

For the last two days, I've gotten a glimpse of what she must be like at work, all proper and organized and full of punctuation and grammar. During the day, her messages are polite, bordering on formal. I can tell she's busy, and I do my best not to bug her too much, but I can't resist firing off the odd inane question, because her responses are so thoughtful and professional.

I, on the other hand, am suddenly aware I can spell or punctuate or create a full sentence, but not all three at once.

And although her daytime efficiency is cute as hell, it's nothing like the Ryan she shows me at night. She's relaxed and flirty and far more open than she is when we're face-to-face. It takes her longer to respond, but when she does, I feel like I'm seeing that side of her I knew was there the moment we met.

I know she sleeps in long-sleeved, white nightgowns because they make her feel elegant. I know she prefers podcasts, doesn't own a television, and can't stand the smell of cinnamon due to her one and only puking-drunk episode during her college years.

I know she's lonely. I know she donates to women's shelters. I know she had one semi-serious boyfriend seven years ago who was a great guy but couldn't compete with her work ethic. I know there's been nothing but a handful of weekend flings since.

I know I'm one of many Doll Parts dates she's had.

And I know I don't like thinking about it.

With our boards prepped, I watch the street corner for a sleek black SUV, my pulse ratcheting up when I finally see one pull over and she steps out. The beach is more crowded than a few days ago, and she takes a moment to scan the area. Her smile is fake until she spots me and it morphs into a reflection of the excitement I'm feeling now that she's here.

Her bag is slung over her shoulder, her chestnut hair pulled back into a ponytail, which swings as she approaches me.

Damn, she's gorgeous.

I've been around women in wetsuits my whole life. They're functional. Yeah, they're tight, but not sexy or revealing like a bikini. Yet Ryan in a wetsuit has my tongue threatening to drop into the sand. I could chalk it up to not getting laid in a couple of months, but the reality is this is Ryan and I haven't found a single thing she does, wears, or says that hasn't turned me on.

Which is a growing problem when I'm dressed in nothing but my board shorts.

"Ready to hit the surf?" I ask as I take her bag from her and nod over to an old friend manning the lifeguard tower. "Carlos will watch over our stuff while we're out there."

She turns toward the tower and waves, giving Carlos a radiant smile. "Thank you for doing this for us!"

And right there, I think I fall a little in love with her.

Once my endorsement money really started rolling in, Cara stopped acknowledging favors done by people she deemed lower on the social hierarchy. Unless someone had the power to amp her own status, they weren't worth the effort of a smile or a kind word. She barely tolerated my friends, Jeremiah being the exception because his name drew crowds almost as big as mine did.

Trying to overcompensate for her rudeness was frustrating and embarrassing. I started to dread those few days she joined me on the beach for anything other than official appearances, knowing my friends would be side-eying me while she paraded around with her phone in hand, taking dozens of selfies until she found the perfect one to post.

I heft a waterproof bag and the boards under my arms, then walk over to the lifeguard station where Ryan is looking up at Carlos and nodding to the advice he's giving about the height of the waves today.

"You aren't trying to scare my girl away from the water, are you?"

"If it'll keep her hanging out with me, you bet I am," he says with a grin. "The sand is safer than the ocean any day, especially when you're riding."

Ryan laughs as I set her board down long enough to flip him off.

"You wish you had my skill in the pocket."

"That I do, Cole. That I do." Winking at Ryan, he straightens up and gets comfortable in his seat. "Have fun out there, you two. And remember there are kids around. Keep it PG."

That flush I adore rises on Ryan's cheeks, and I'd buy Carlos a beer after his shift if I wasn't still feeling a little jealous over his obvious appreciation of Ryan in her suit.

She scoops up her board before I can, and we fall into step toward the water.

"That's twice I've heard people call you Cole. Do you prefer it over Malcolm?"

"Malcolm is what I go by everywhere but out here," I reply as we leash up. "Cole is more of a nickname."

Or my pro name, the one people who follow the surfing circuit would recognize. Around here Cole Sullivan is a household name, made famous thanks to my talent and made infamous thanks to what was deemed a career-ending injury.

I know I should be upfront about it with her, but admitting who I used to be opens the door to questions I don't want to answer, questions I've been avoiding for the past year.

Of course, all she has to do is search my pro name and she'll see everything up to the moment I dropped out of the limelight. Hiding it is likely to make it more of an issue, and the fact is I like her. A lot. I want her to trust me and know me. I want to bring her deeper into this little slice of ocean heaven I have for as long as I have it. It's why I've met her here at my beach and not farther down the coast.

I want her on my turf.

But opening up to her doesn't mean sharing every gory detail.

Decision made, I step into the water and fasten my

bag tight to my back. "Ready?"

"Is anyone ever really ready to face death?"

Her expression can only be described as fierce as she stares the ocean down and walks at my side through the shallow surf. When she flattens on her board and paddles out, I see a confidence she didn't have on her first venture. Her strokes are stronger, longer, and more deliberate, and I know despite her words, she's not afraid to face the waves with me.

We manage to ride four in before her first fall, and I'm amazed at the improvement in her pop-up.

"You've been practicing," I say as we paddle out again. "I'm insanely impressed right now."

She wrinkles her nose. "I hate not being good at something, so I've been doing one hundred pop-ups a day and watching how-to videos before bed every night."

And I fall a little deeper.

I lead her to a quieter area where the strength of the waves is dampened by a natural rise in the ocean floor. Waiting until she's beside me, I remove my leash and tether our boards together.

"Dinner time."

Her brows shoot up as I sling my backpack off and start pulling out the meal I put together earlier.

"Dinner? Out here, where the sharks live?"

"Right above them," I reply with a grin. "You have your choice of wraps: southwestern, Caesar, BLT, or an Italian chicken concoction my friend Wade got me hooked on a few years ago."

Licking her lips, she peers over the edge of her board for a moment before straightening up. "BLT, please."

I pass over the wrap and a bottle of water then grab the Italian chicken. "This is probably as good a time as any to tell you I used to be a professional surfer."

Her eyes widen for a moment before they narrow, and she lasers me with an accusatory glare. "You could have said something earlier so I'd stop trying to prove I could be better than you."

"You're close."

"Don't patronize me," she huffs before her feigned indignation gives way. "Seriously, though? That's really cool. Were you good or really good?"

"The best."

The words still feel wrong, like I lost the right to say them when my career came to a sudden end.

Ryan's expression shifts from impressed to curious, and I brace myself.

"When did you stop competing?"

"One year ago next week. I was going in for an aerial in my final wave for what should have been a win a few hours north of here." I take a deep breath and feel the familiar ache in my knee. "I've seen the video footage, and to this day, I don't know where I went wrong. All I know is one second I was riding and the next I was ragdolling in the water. By the time I was pulled out, I'd torn my ACL and damaged two other ligaments in my right knee. I looked like I'd lost a bar fight against a dozen MMA champions." Shrugging to shake off the heaviness, I stretch my leg out so she can see the scars. "Surgery and rehab could only go so far. But the good news is I lived."

She reaches over and grazes her fingers along the most jagged scar. "I can't imagine how hard it must have been for you."

I can feel the heat of her skin as her hand skims along the white remnants of my surgeries, and for the first time, those scars feel less like marks of failure and more like badges. Of what, I don't know yet. "It's been a rough few months," I confess. "Once I dug myself out of the self-pity trench I was in, I realized I needed to move on with the next stage of my life."

"And what does this next stage involve?" she asks with a smile, patting my knee before scooting back to the middle of her board.

Pointing toward the boardwalk where Barreled's sign is unreadable at this distance, I swallow another bite of my wrap. "See the surf shop over there? I'm saving up to buy it. I practically grew up between those aisles and on the water, so I figure owning the store is the next best thing if I can't get back on the circuit."

"I love it." She sighs with a wistfulness in her voice. "I can't imagine anything better than working here all day. Fresh air, beautiful views...so much better than office walls with windows overlooking the eleven coffee shops I can count from my desk."

I gaze out into the broad expanse of the ocean where the waves roll rhythmically toward shore. "To be honest, I don't know what I'll do if I can't come up with the money to buy it. Wade and Emma are the owners, and because of them, Barreled was more of a home for me than my real one ever was." The blatant honesty I'm spewing out isn't like me, but I can't seem to stop. "It's going to be tough enough when those two are gone. The thought of not being able to continue their legacy out here is—" I pause and swallow before letting out a long exhale. "I just hope I can make it work before someone else swoops in and destroys everything that made Barreled what it is."

Ryan is quiet for so long I start to second-guess how

much I shared with a woman who pays for dates to avoid the whole entanglement thing. We may have been opening up more over texts for the past few days, but face-to-face is a whole other ballgame.

"What if you can't get the money fast enough?" she asks quietly, and I look over to see her staring at the horizon.

Of course she went for the question keeping me up at night.

What if?

What if the extra hours I'm putting in with Doll Parts aren't enough? What if sacrificing my time on the waves to pad my bank account means I screw up any chance I have of a comeback to the pro circuit?

What if I lose both?

And no one—not even Jeremiah—knows I'm gunning for a return to competition. Every dime I earn is tied up saving to buy Barreled, leaving nothing for proper rehab or trainers. It's all on me, and what's left of my pride won't let me fail in front of anyone again.

Shrugging, I pack everything back into my bag and seal it. "I have no plan B. It's Barreled or bust. I have three months."

Something in her expression shifts from contemplative to bothered, and it stays like that for the rest of the date.

Chapter Eight

Ryan

Renna stands in my office with her arms crossed, reminding me why best friends shouldn't work together.

"Nothing?" she echoes, her gold eyeshadow glinting in the sun coming through the window as her eyes narrow on me. "Two dates and you still have no idea why he needs money so bad? No hint? No red flags? No sixth sense?"

I send off a firm yet polite email refusing a request to merge with another man-for-rent company on the east coast, power off my laptop, and close it. "Nothing. Malcolm is a closed book, but I don't think his finances are anything we need to be worried about."

I've been fighting an internal battle for the two days it's been since I had a dinner date on the ocean. Putting Renna's mind at ease would be simple. I could easily reassure her he isn't drowning in a gambling debt or running from a drug dealer, but what he told me felt so intensely personal I can't bring myself to share the intel.

Renna's eyes glaze over for a moment, letting me know her brain is working overtime. "Then we need to shift gears. Maybe meeting him on his turf is the wrong approach. Tomorrow, we bring him to yours."

My hands go clammy with the thought of being exposed. "I don't think dragging him to another black tie event is the way to push for an intimate conversation," I argue, applauding myself for making such a rational rebuttal while my heart is pounding in my ears. "Perhaps we should consider extending the booking times, blocking off a whole afternoon and evening. I have the feeling he begins to check out toward the end of our dates because he has to prepare for another one the same night."

It isn't a total lie. Although Malcolm seemed almost regretful when we said our goodbyes before sunset, he and I both knew he was on his way out for another booking within the hour. And after his revelation out on the water, a discomfort definitely settled over us.

Though if I'm being honest, I caused it. Hearing him admit he had no backup plan if he couldn't earn enough to buy the surf shop had my head sinking into the very thoughts Renna was worried about.

He has a motive to break Doll Parts's rules.

A big motive.

A motive I can understand no matter how much thinking about him crossing that invisible line to ensure he makes his deadline nauseates me.

Brows furrowed, Renna taps away on her phone in silence while I text my driver and double-check my calendar.

"Done. I shuffled his date with Rowena Cutler out of tomorrow's time slot and blocked the whole day and night under your name." She mutters under her breath before sliding her cell into the pocket of her pinup-style red dress. "Brit asked me to remind you to submit your receipts for these dates so she can enter them into coaching expenses."

"I will," I lie, knowing I'll need to come up with an

excuse soon. "Let me know if any issues arise tonight, and I'll update you on Malcolm once I'm home tomorrow."

Leaving her to lock up, I ride the elevator down and beeline to the awaiting car. I mumble my thanks and raise the privacy glass as my driver eases the car door shut behind me.

Submitting receipts for dates with Malcolm is yet another ethical issue I'm facing. The longer I avoid it, the more I open myself up for questions from both Renna and Brit. But to do so feels wrong, like I'm betraying him even more than I already have.

Staring out the tinted window, I try to catch a glimpse of the ocean between the high-rises and come up empty.

I know he isn't on the water this evening. He's attending an invite-only party in the hills, and judging from the pictures his date is uploading on her social media account, he's doing a damn good job being her right-hand man.

Because it's his job.

A job I've employed him to do.

Knocking the back of my head against the seat a few times, I let out a low groan of frustration.

I've never tracked my employees the way I track Malcolm. I know his job description thanks to the hours I spent writing and tweaking it, but that doesn't matter. Seeing him snuggled up to other women is like my own personal version of torture porn, and I can't bring myself to look away.

He's a car accident on the highway, and I'm scrolling like the twisted rubbernecker I am while my driver weaves through traffic to bring me to a date of my own.

I can feel my business mask slip back into place as we pull up to a restaurant on the west side. Tonight, I'm test-driving a potential employee Renna has decided will fit the roughneck vacancy she discovered during one of her impromptu client polls. His credentials are impeccable, his appearance the polar opposite of Malcolm with a shock of black hair, a beard, and enough ink to put some lucky tattooist's kid through Yale.

Spotting my date waiting outside, I thank my driver, get out, and get my head in the game.

****

Malcolm

I can feel Jeremiah's eyes on me from my kitchen as I watch the clock.

"Stop with the pacing already," he mumbles, his mouth full of the hummus I was hoping he wouldn't find hiding behind the expired sour cream. "You're acting like this is an actual date and you're fourteen again."

"Fuck off."

It's the only thing I trust myself to say, because technically, yeah, it's another Doll Parts job.

But it's Ryan.

Ryan from noon until midnight.

Pausing in front of the living room window overlooking the Pacific, I clear my throat and run my hand through my hair.

A lot can happen in twelve hours, and I spent all last night fantasizing about pretty much every way we could fill the time before she sent me a detailed itinerary at two in the morning.

Jeremiah makes himself at home on my sofa and turns on the TV. "I hope you know the day you get rid of your streaming services is the day we break up."

"I'm counting on it," I reply, too distracted by the ticking clock to put any effort into a decent comeback. "I want you gone by seven, and I want it as clean as it was ten minutes before your sand-crusted ass showed up."

A wide grin spreads across his face. "Holy shit, I knew those towels in the bathroom looked fresh. And you changed your sheets, didn't you?"

"Fuck off."

"Why would you want me gone by seven if you're supposed to be playing the arm-candy role for some hard-up chick all night?" he presses, biting down on the tidbit of information I inadvertently supplied like a dog with a bone. "And didn't you say there's a no-boning clause?"

Shoving my keys, wallet, and phone into the pockets of my cargo shorts, I shoot him a warning glare on my way out the door. "Seven. Spotless."

"Aye, aye, Romeo."

I'm meeting Ryan at a coffeehouse a few blocks away from Doll Parts, and as I near my destination, I can't help but look around at every office building and condo complex I pass, wondering which—if any—are hers. The area is sleek, all new construction of metal and mirrored glass. Fountains and manicured gardens grace a few of the terraces in a weak attempt to bring some of ocean into the metropolis, but I can already sense the change in the air before I even step out of my truck.

This was one of the areas Cara was eying when my bank account began to swell. She was drawn to the shine, to the promise of nightlife and wealth and a life insulated from everything—and everyone—she deemed unpleasant. Initially, I'd pushed against the idea of moving away from the ocean. But I caved when she guilted me with reminders of my grueling competition schedule and the long weeks she would spend alone.

As far as I know, she's still living two blocks over in the overpriced penthouse my most lucrative board endorsement paid for.

My phone buzzes, and I answer it with a smile, thinking it must be Ryan.

It isn't.

"Hey, babe," coos the devil I conjured with my internal musings. "Whatcha doing?"

Slumping back in my seat, I press my palm to my forehead to relieve the influx of pressure building. "What do you want, Cara?"

"I just wanted to hear your voice," she replies.

I swear I can hear the pout she's putting on while she continues talking like we didn't split on the nastiest of terms.

"Matty said he saw you out on the waves this morning. Said you were looking real good. Like, competition-level good."

My hackles rise. "You heard wrong. I'll ask again, Cara, and then I'm hanging up. What do you want?"

There's a heavy sigh, and I can picture her lounging on the angular chrome-and-white sofa she insisted we buy despite how uncomfortable it was to sit on.

"I miss you. I thought you might miss me, too." Her voice drops into a familiar seductive purr. "I want to see you and take care of you. Maybe we could take care of each other."

I wait for the pain to hit, but all I feel is irritation. Irritation with a hefty dose of self-loathing for welcoming this woman into my life and giving her the power to wreck me all those months ago.

I was such a fucking idiot.

Maybe I still am.

On edge and annoyed, I check the time to see I'm now two minutes late. "Not a chance in hell. Tell your husband I say hi."

I hang up and take a deep breath to shake Cara's voice from my head. Remnants of the former neighborhood are few and far between in this rejuvenated concrete jungle, the quaint coffee shop being one of them. I spot Ryan through the large windows immediately. Her presence is a homing beacon, and I come to a stop outside the doors to watch her for a moment, to recenter myself.

While most of the patrons are outfitted in muted designer labels and carrying purses I know for a fact cost more than most people make in a week, Ryan looks like she belongs in this rustic little cafe. There's nothing fake about her, no airs put on in her movements. Her hair is pulled up in a simple ponytail, its sway leading my eyes down to the black tank top hugging her curves and showing off the dip of her waist. I drink in the flare of her hips where a long black-and-white skirt hangs low, hiding her amazing legs until she turns, and the asymmetrical hemline brings my gaze to rest on the juncture of her thighs.

When I snap out of the hypnotic thoughts of what lies inches above that fabric, I scan the patrons and realize I'm not the only one noticing the delectable vision that damn skirt provides. My unwelcome phone call forgotten, I make my way to her, slide a possessive arm around her waist, and level a glare at the boldest guy eyeballing her. "I take it you're testing my bodyguard abilities today?"

She looks up at me with a flash of fear before her expression schools. "Testing?"

Making sure she sees just how much I do truly appreciate the view, I take my time raking my gaze over her. "Well, yeah. When you look this hot, the likelihood of me brawling with some overconfident, perverted asshole doubles. I figure you did this on purpose to see if a certified beach bum can hold his own against a metropolitan gym rat in a fight for your honor."

She blinks a few times before the smile I didn't even realize I'd been desperate to see makes an appearance.

"Now that you mention it, I am a little curious who would win."

My grip on her tightens a fraction, and she laughs, her body turning toward mine.

"Did you get my plan for the day?"

"The color-coded hourly breakdown with the alternative options for everything highlighted in orange?" A flush rises on her cheeks, and I grin. "Your obsessive organization is strangely attractive."

With a little huff, she untangles herself from my hold and moves up to the front place in line. "Organization is important."

"And sexy," I add while she orders her coffee, some raspberry-chocolate contraption that sounds a little too sweet for my taste.

I place my own request for the largest, most caffeinated cup they have, we step aside, and she pulls out her phone.

"I tweaked it more on the way here. I'm a little worried the wait at the botanical garden could be long, but I suppose we can cut the gallery visit short if we have to so we aren't late to the Shakespeare in the Park event."

I have a flashback to Glenda, the PR woman who herded me from place to place during the height of my career. Except I don't remember getting hard when Glenda went over my schedule for the day. My dick's reaction to the way Ryan bites her lower lip while she reviews the inputted drive times should worry me because although I've been turned on by a few weird things over the years, spreadsheets have never made the list until today.

Reading over her shoulder, I frown at the last line, which is written in all caps and highlighted in red, a line she didn't include when she sent the itinerary to me.

12:00 TIMER SET. SIGN OFF ON APP. LEAVE STARRED REVIEW.

Like everything else on her list, there's a blank box for her to check, something she does to the first entry as our names are called to retrieve our coffee.

And I suddenly feel, for lack of a better word, cheap.

Bought.

Which yeah, technically, I am. And the rate definitely isn't cheap.

But knowing Ryan is paying to see me hits differently when I see it confirmed in writing. It leaves a faint blemish on every memory I have of the woman who's occupying more and more of my thoughts day and night. She may have bent Doll Parts rules and given me her number, but I suddenly can't shake the suspicion it's part of a game and I'm setting myself up to be played.

We slip through the line to an empty table along the wall and slide into the booth side by side, the silence becoming uncomfortable the longer it stretches out.

"How was the rest of your weekend?"

I snap out of the blank stare down I was having with the table. "How old are you?"

Her lips purse, and she leans against the padded bench. "Thirty-six."

I may not have done too well in school, but I figure out the eleven-year difference pretty fast. She and Cara are the same age, and the unwelcome emotions accompanying that particular piece of information drive the next words out of my mouth. "So I take it you've got a thing for younger guys?"

There's a harshness to my voice, and an apology is on the tip of my tongue, but I can't spit it out.

Her reply is a simple lift of her brows, so my dumb self barrels ahead.

"Have you ever been married?"

I don't even know why I'm asking these questions, why I'm opening myself up to the inevitable fair-game turnaround. Having the "past relationships" talk isn't casual client-employee conversation, but I go there anyway.

Maybe I have unexplored masochistic tendencies.

She gives me a look telling me she's as surprised by my hard tone as I am. "No. I have no hangup about younger guys. I've never been married, I have no kids, I don't have time for pets, and I don't own any houseplants. I work, Malcolm. I work and I read."

"And hire dates."

Holy fuck, I've flown straight over Jerk Land and parked my tantruming, angsty ass on Bastard Island.

"Yes," she replies tersely before she takes a long a sip of her cooling coffee. "And I hire dates because they usually comprehend the parameters."

Her body language shifts gears. Gone is the relaxed

tilt of her head and the subtle lean toward me. She crosses her legs, putting a few extra inches between us before setting her cup down and squaring her shoulders. The warmth in her eyes morphs into a stoic, unaffected ice. "I think I missed something between the time you arrived and the time we sat down."

"Just making sure we both know what we're doing here." I down my coffee in one gulp, regretting it the moment it burns my throat. "Done. What's next on the docket?"

If I didn't feel like a totally irredeemable dick thirty seconds ago, I sure as hell do when she takes a sip, sets her cup down, and stands.

"Thank you for coming out this afternoon, Mr. Sullivan, but I've decided I prefer my own company to this lovely, condescending inquisition. Enjoy your day off."

Chapter Nine

Ryan

There are many things in this world I don't do.
I don't gamble.
I don't eat cottage cheese in any form.
I don't wear shoes with pointed toes.
And I don't cry.

Which means I'm extra disoriented and upset when I find myself storming across the street with tears threatening to spill down my cheeks.

Tears. Actual tears. Actual goddamn tears because of a man.

Once I'm out of sight of the coffee shop, I take a shaky breath and release it, finding my center as I internalize my new mantra for the day.

Screw. Malcolm. Sullivan.

I repeat the words in my head as I walk along to the steady cadence toward the row of cabs parked ahead.

Screw. Malcolm. Sullivan.

It has a nice ring to it, a steady rhythm I can focus on as I get my bearings and make a decision.

I'm going on this date.

And I'm ordering—and eating—two desserts because Screw Malcolm Sullivan.

His turnabout was so sudden I debate booking an appointment with the acupuncturist who slipped me his card during a fundraiser last December, because there's a good chance I strained something whipping my head back and forth.

I slide into the first taxi available, give him the address of the botanical garden, and relax back in the slightly sticky pleather seat as I sail past the surprise and hurt of earlier and settle into indignation.

He had no right to speak to me the way he did, his accusatory tone lashing at me while he drilled me. Doll Parts compensates him very well to not be an asshole. If basic respect didn't stay his tongue, the money should have.

The cab takes a sharp corner, and I tighten my hold on my purse.

Screw Malcolm Sullivan.

Any worry I had about placing him on a pedestal or being blinded by his shiny exterior has been squashed. Temperamental men are a dime a dozen, and most won't cost my business a thousand dollars to suss out.

Huffing, I purse my lips and stare out the window because I'm glad this happened. Glad, glad, glad. All the dishonesty and sneakiness is over, and I'm no worse for wear because that red flag waved big and bright in the coffee house.

The entrance to the botanical garden comes into view, and I prepare to pay for my ride, reminding myself today is not a total write-off because I need the self-care an untethered day will provide. I've earned it. I deserve it. And I don't need a man with me to enjoy myself. I never did before.

Resolve steeled, I pay the driver and walk into the garden, taking a map of the grounds as I enter and compare the recommended tour with one I created last night.

Step one, roses.

Within minutes I'm so caught up in admiring an arch of delicate yellow blooms I don't notice anyone closing in on me until an arm brushes against mine.

"I'm sorry."

His voice is low and repentant enough to chip the glass wall my Screw Malcolm Sullivan mantra erected on the drive here. I say nothing and continue to take in the beauty of the rose garden, walking the narrow path with him following half a step behind until we reach the tulip beds and his hand skims mine.

"Ryan."

My emotions are going in reverse, resolve giving way to ire before stalling out in a hurt I try to cover with practiced aloofness. "Please don't feel obligated to be here," I say, wrapping my fingers over the cool metal bar separating the walkway from the display. "I won't lodge a complaint or do anything to affect your ratings."

"I don't give a rat's ass about my ratings," he states, mimicking my position and staring out at the colorful field. "I care about apologizing because I was a complete jerk to you and you didn't deserve it."

The glass wall shatters in one corner, making it vulnerable.

I glance up at him for a second before looking back to the tulips and nudging his shoulder gently with mine. "Apology accepted if you tell me why."

His pinky finger hooks over mine. When I don't tug away, he takes my hand and leads me toward the perennials. "My ex-wife called just as I arrived at the shop, and I answered, thinking it was you."

Ex-wife.

Words abandon me as I try to imagine what kind of supermodel siren a guy like Malcolm would rush to marry when he was so young. "Oh."

"Yeah, oh." He sighs, shoving his free hand through his hair. "If anyone can bring my asshole side out, it's her. Unfortunately, you were the collateral damage, and I'm sorry."

I hear his repeated apology but can't move past the pertinent information. "You're divorced."

"Finalized in April."

Phrases like "on the rebound" and "sowing his wild oats" flash through my mind, and I ease my fingers out of his loose hold. "You've only been divorced for two months."

Frowning, he scoops my hand up again. "Hey. Don't."

My laugh is nervous and forced, a holdover defense from my college years when I would find myself outside of my comfort zone. I worm out of his reach and walk a little faster, unfolding the map as I do so and gripping it with both hands. "I've heard the lily display is lacking until later in the season, so maybe the vineyard would be a good end to the tour since we'd have to travel through the Asian garden to get there."

"Ryan."

I look up and give him the smile I've hidden behind hundreds of times. "Yes?"

His jaw is clenched, and the muscles flex under his scruff. "What bothers you more, me being divorced or how much of an ass I was to you because I'm an idiot?"

"Neither," I say, keeping my voice neutrally cheery. "You apologized, I accepted. Nothing about our situation is remotely affected by your past relationships."

He stays by my side in silence as we walk through the incredible show the Asian flowers produce. I take a few pictures to distract myself from his presence, his mere proximity wreaking havoc on the calm exterior I'm desperately clinging to.

When we reach the grand arches of the vineyard, he joins me under a veil of wisteria blossoms, his hands shoved deep in his pockets. "See the guy standing over there by the brick wall?"

I take a moment to spot him. "Yeah?"

"He met his ex-wife when he was twenty-one and she was thirty-two. He was a top-tier lacrosse player who had just signed his first endorsement deal when this gorgeous, sophisticated woman came up to him and introduced herself."

I know I'm not going to like this story, but my curiosity is piqued. "Did he fall in love at first sight?"

Scoffing, Malcolm leans against a wrought iron arch wrapped in pink clematis flowers. "He fell in lust at first sight. She gave off this uptown, worldly vibe, always dressed like she just stepped off a runway. And he was just a dumb jock with a mediocre high school education trying to play against pros with secondhand equipment."

He lets out a long puff of air. "His career was taking off, so when she moved in after a month, it seemed right because everything else in his life was moving so fast. Two months later, they were hunting for condos."

With no frame of reference of my own, I nod to let him know I'm listening.

"They fought constantly," he states without emotion, crossing his arms and fixing his gaze on a climbing rose. "But because he also traveled constantly, he didn't realize how bad it was when he was home.

After a while, his girlfriend wasn't happy with free access to his credit card. She wanted a ring. So he proposed and they eloped. He added her to his bank accounts shortly after." His tone shifts, the bitterness at odds with his usually carefree demeanor. "A few months later, he had a career-ending accident on the field and found himself laid up in the hospital with no lacrosse career, no endorsements, no wife, and no money."

"Fuck that," I growl before slapping my hand over my mouth, like it will erase the curse I just spat out.

"My sentiments exactly."

****

Malcolm

The last thing I want is pity, so when outrage is Ryan's first reaction to the story of my failed marriage I've managed to project onto a poor sap waiting for his mom, some of the tension in my shoulders releases.

She wraps her arms around herself, her delicate brows furrowed. "Is he okay now? The lacrosse player?"

It's easier to talk about it through some random stranger who has no idea Ryan and I are using him as a medium for my sad-sack tale. "He's getting there," I say, deciding I've already gone this far, so I might as well go for gold. "He met a hot human resources director he's crazy about, he's saving to buy a lacrosse supply store, and he's training for a pro comeback. Things are getting better as long as he doesn't fuck it all by being a dumbass."

Her head snaps up, and her eyes go wide. "A comeback? For real?"

"Yeah, for real," I say before swallowing with the admission and stretching out my knee instinctively. "It's not a guarantee I'll be able to do it, but I can try, right?"

She presses her palms to my chest, and her fingers dance a little beat against me as she smiles up at me with unrestrained excitement. "That's incredible, Malcolm! How long have you been training? Is your knee holding up? Did you get a doctor's approval?" Her enthusiasm is replaced by concern as the gears churn in her head. "When do you even have the time? When are you hoping to make your return? Shouldn't you be practicing right now?"

"Three months, yes, meh, early mornings, August, and no," I reply with a chuckle, taking her hands in mine and turning them up to kiss her palms before placing them back where I want them. "Ryan, I know I've said it twice, but I really am sorry I took things out on you. I let shit from my past ruin what should have been an amazing day for us."

I can't help but follow the movement of her tongue as she licks her lips and inhales.

"Okay, but your knee—"

"Is going to be fine. The real question is are we going to be fine?"

If I wasn't so desperate to hear a yes, I would find her worried glance down to my knee endearing, but me and patience aren't traveling in the same car right now. I tip her chin up and force her to look at me. "Ryan."

"Is there a we?" she asks, her hands still warming my chest.

"Damn right there is."

Unable to wait any longer, I dip my head down and brush my lips against hers, keeping it light until she sways a fraction closer and her nails dig into my shirt. Green-lighted, I wrap my hand around the nape of her neck and swipe my tongue along the seam of her mouth, groaning when she opens for me.

She tastes like raspberry chocolate coffee, and I take back every thought I had about it being too sweet. It's perfect. Delicious. Addictive. Combine it with her hands sliding up the column of my throat and into my hair, and I'm an insta-junkie for this woman. I get the same sensation of ragdolling in the waves, being tossed head over ass time and time again until I don't know up from down. Her body presses against mine as our tongues tangle, and I can't remember why we haven't been doing this since the night we met.

Someone clears their throat behind me, and I huff as Ryan ducks her head and hides in the crook of my neck.

"Yeah, yeah." I grunt, giving the woman dragging two disinterested kids along the evil eye before smoothing my hands over Ryan's ribs and settling them on her hips. "She only wishes someone would kiss her like that."

Ryan laughs silently into my shirt, and I feel lighter than I have in ages.

Chapter Ten

Ryan

Last night was, without a doubt, the best date I've had in my life, and I can't tell a damn soul.

I don't even own a plant I can gush to about it.

Nothing at this catered businesswoman's luncheon can compare to the mint-and-mango taste of Malcolm's lips when he kissed me breathless under the stars during Shakespeare in the Park while Lady MacBeth washed her sins from her hands. Not even the raspberry torte.

I'm struggling to focus on the speeches, dragged from my blissful daydreams every time polite applause fills the air. All I can think about is the feeling of Malcolm's hand sliding along the slit of my dress under the table during dinner, stopping just shy of being indecent and staying there throughout the duration of our meal.

"So what did you learn?" Renna whisper-yells beside me, and I startle, realizing the keynote speaker has taken the podium.

Blinking, I try to review the past ten minutes for a clue about what she means. "A lot."

Something in my tone has her frowning. "That bad?"

Bad. Bad. Oh, right.

I wasn't on that date with Malcolm to find out how

intense a kisser he can be when my driver is running ten minutes late and he's taking it as a personal challenge to get me revved up before I head home. I had a mission. Deciding vague is the best approach, I shake my head and lean close to her. "Not at all. He's saving to buy a little shop on the waterfront. Nothing we need to concern ourselves with."

Renna is visibly relieved as she slouches back in her seat. "Thank God, because that stallion is becoming our most in-demand employee."

The banquet hall suddenly feels a little warm, a bit claustrophobic.

I excuse myself, slip from the room, and take the elevator to the open-aired rooftop atrium. The glass surrounds shelter me from the winds, and I take a seat on a bench overlooking the ocean, squinting at the waves as though I might be able to make him out from this distance.

And I know I'm in deep. Maybe too deep.

Visions of my mother dancing around the kitchen with stars in her eyes surge to the forefront of my mind. How many times did she spin and twirl and clap her hands to her heart, proclaiming she'd found true love? I'm not delusional enough to believe Malcolm and I are anywhere close to it, but I can't ignore the signs of infatuation I'm exhibiting, the signs I learned to watch for every time my mom returned from another first date.

My phone buzzes, and I swipe it to life, answering his call on the first ring and mentally ticking my eagerness off the growing warnings list in my head. "Hey."

"Hey yourself," he says, a teasing tone in his voice. "Shouldn't you be working?"

"Shouldn't you be training?" I counter with a smile.

I can hear the gentle lapping of water and the telltale sound of seagulls squawking in the background.

"I'm out here right now," he says, and my phone vibrates as a photo fills my screen. "The view is incredible. Ditch work and meet me on the shore."

The offer is tempting. So tempting.

Too tempting.

The picture he sent shows the tip of his board pointed toward the vast expanse of the ocean where gentle whitecaps dot the cerulean-blue water. Puffs of white clouds float above the horizon, and I sigh, smelling the salty breeze while the sound of cars and horns hum from the street below.

He must sense my hesitation because his voice takes on a cajoling lilt. "Come on, Ryan. Play hooky. Just this once."

Just this once.

I'm already walking to the elevator before I realize what I'm doing. "I'll be there in thirty."

****

Malcolm

I don't think I could get any higher than I am right now.

Ryan's board slips under the wave with her on it, paddling furiously to catch the swells cresting ahead of us. Thanks to the heat of the day, she's wearing nothing but a black one-piece bathing suit she bought on the boardwalk minutes after she arrived at the beach, and I can't tear my gaze off the high cut framing her ass.

It's a perfect day to be on the water, made even better by her smile as she pops up and rides all the way in. Six hours of training has me moving slower, but I sure can't complain when I'm treated to the sight of her doubling back toward me every time she catches a wave I miss.

"If anyone asks, I'm home sick with a headache," she calls with a grin, her long hair slicked back in a ponytail and showing off her kissable throat. "Can you believe I almost didn't come?"

Grabbing her board as she closes in on me, I steady her and lean in for a taste of her lips. "Good thing you did because my next plan of attack involved kidnapping and ropes."

Her breathing hitches, and suddenly surfing is my second-choice activity for the rest of the afternoon. Trusting my leash to keep my board from going AWOL on me, I cross over onto hers, laughing when she flattens down and grasps the sides.

"Have you ever made out on the water?" I ask with a smirk as she shifts slowly onto her back. "I've heard it's mind-blowing."

"Oh you heard, did you?" she counters, arching her head back when I dip my head down to kiss her neck. "We're going to tip off."

I silence her warning with my mouth and tongue, pressing my hips between her thighs when she lets go of the board and wraps her arms around my shoulders.

Balancing against the roll of the ocean is as instinctual for me as breathing. With Ryan warm and pliant beneath me and the waves rocking under us, I'm riding a euphoria I didn't think was possible. Her skin tastes like salt water, and I want to devour every inch. Too many surfers are still out here for me to risk anything more than a little over-the-suit groping, but I'm sure not going to complain.

"One of these nights, I'm going to fuck you out here on this board," I growl, sliding my hand between her thighs and touching her over the smooth spandex of her bathing suit.

Her laugh is a mixture of surprise and indulgence, but a nervousness is in her voice when she speaks. "You want to induct me into your surfer version of the Mile High Club?"

Being careful to avoid shifting my weight too quickly, I crawl up her body and brace my hands on either side of her head so I can look down at her. "Well, yeah. It would be hot as hell."

Her eyes shift toward shore. "You don't think it would be a little, I don't know, risky?"

Nipping at her throat, I shake my head. "It's, like, surfer fantasy number two, right after sweeping the season." I trail my lips along her jaw. "Think about it. You and me at sunset, you looking all smoking gorgeous in an easy-access bikini—"

"With sharks and spectators," she interjects, her hips lifting a fraction when I grind my aching cock against her.

I can feel her heat through my board shorts and the fluttering of her pulse, but I know she isn't there yet, even before she confirms it with her words.

"It sounds dangerous and a little, um, scary."

As bad as I want to say fuck the sunset and show her just how good I'm positive board sex would be, I don't want her feeling uncertain in any way the first time we sleep together. I want her relaxed and eager and unrestrained. I want her to want me so much she forgets her lists and schedules and timetables. I want her to want me as badly as I want her.

"The danger will be half the fun," I say as I kiss the tip of her nose and sit back on my haunches while a group of rookies paddles by. "Why don't we head in? We can go back to my place, order dinner, and just hide out for the rest of the day."

One nod from her is all it takes for me to hop off her board and mount mine, staying at her back while we ride in so none of the rookies tries to hone in on her wave.

"Do you live close?" she asks when I join her on the beach, her leash already undone and her board under her arm.

I take her free hand in mine, nodding to Carlos as I scoop up our bags and sling them over my shoulder. "You could say that. I rent the apartment above Barreled."

She turns toward the shop and smiles, her eyes lighting up. "You actually live right here on the beach? Like, right here?"

"Like right here," I echo with a chuckle. "The apartment is part of the sale, so I have even more motivation than most buyers would."

I'm practically pulled across the sand as she drags me to the steps leading to my small balcony overlooking the ocean. There's no time for me to worry about what kind of mess I left early this morning, because I'm too focused on watching while she climbs up the wooden staircase and stops at the top to admire the view.

Her expression shifts from excitement to a reflection of the same humbled awe I experience every time I step out my front door.

I fall a tad more for her.

She's silent as she looks across the coastline, her gaze drifting farther out over the swimmers and surfers to the ships on the horizon. Her fingers grip the railing a bit tighter, and she takes a deep breath, closing her eyes. "You can't lose this."

I open my door and hang both boards in the hall to buy myself a moment because she's right and I don't want to think about it. "I won't."

With one last inhale of the ocean air, she follows me inside for the grand tour of the two-bedroom, two-bathroom apartment. While Cara despised the rustic, beachy feel of the place, Ryan sees what I see in it. She marvels over the enormous windows providing the best view in the state and moans with appreciation of the clawfoot tub. Even her obsession over the exposed-beam ceilings rivals my own.

But her reaction when I take her through a narrow stairwell up to the roof makes me realize the two of us are more alike than I ever imagined.

Surrounded by cheap plastic furniture and oversized pots filled with sturdy, drought-resistant cactuses, she takes a tentative step close to the unfenced edge and sighs. "I never understood how people can say they've fallen in love with a building, but I get it now."

Taking her hand and tugging her back gently so I don't have a heart attack over the possibility of her falling, I lead her to the lounge chair. "You haven't seen anything yet. Sit here."

She obeys, reclining back as I crouch beside her. From this angle, no one else exists. The view is nothing but water and sky and birds, the din of noise below buffered enough to fade into the background.

"Malcolm?"

"Yeah?"

Her eyes harden as she stares out at the waves. "You have to make this happen."

Chapter Eleven

Ryan

I'm a pillar of steel, unbreakable and unyielding.
I cannot be swayed.
I will not be moved.
I am strength and power and resolve.

Touching up my lipstick in my office en suite, I square my shoulders and admire my unwavering fortitude because I've held strong for thirteen days and I will not break.

I will not cave to the temptation to answer my phone when it rings.

I will not respond to texts until a minimum of two hours has passed.

I will not ask my driver to take the ocean-view drive instead of the freeways.

What I will do is continue to stack Malcolm's schedule with back-to-back dates, because what he has to lose is worth a hell of a lot more than my selfish desire to monopolize his time.

"Cody needed to back out of Savannah Porter's ribbon cutting at seven," Renna hollers at me through the door. "I can shuffle Terrence in, but he's been on the golf course with Marianna all day and might not want to attend a six-hour formal."

I exit the bathroom, open up the master spreadsheet

of appointments, and scour it for a solution. "Put Terrence in Malcolm's place for Abby's basketball game and shift Malcolm into Cody's spot."

I can see Renna completing the changes in real time while I start calling clients to ensure they approve the switch-ups. Reassuring Abby her new date is, in fact, a basketball fan who won't judge her face paint, I fire off confirmations of the adjustments to the guys.

"This pushes Malcolm to sixty hours for the week," Renna says as she saunters into my office and takes a seat on the sofa. "I know you approved him going above the recommended number of jobs, but don't you think this may be a little too much? We don't want to burn him out when he's such a draw."

"If we keep him busy earning legitimate money, the chance of him going rogue for other sources drops," I state. "The last thing we need is our top earner gaining a reputation for providing unapproved services. And you know all it takes is one time for the rumors to start."

Renna sighs. "I know. He just looked exhausted when he came by this morning an—"

"What do you mean, when he came by?" I demand, my pulse shooting through the roof. "Why was he here?"

I'm mentally running through every time I opened my office door over the last four hours while my best friend shrugs.

"He dropped off some surf instructor certification papers. I'm telling you, though, he looked rough. Not partied-all-night rough. More like rushed-and-stressed-and-unhappy rough." She side-eyes me like she can tell my palms have become damp. "Like you do."

Scoffing, I make a small tweak to my schedule to avoid too much overlap. "I look like I always do."

With her attention drawn to her phone, she rolls her eyes. "I know."

I mutter a few choice words her way and ease my compact mirror from my purse to assess my face in the sunlight streaming through my windows.

"To be fair," Renna continues while completely ignoring my crisis of eye-bag proportions, "those surf dates you were going on with Malcolm over the last couple of weeks did wonders for the whole businesswoman-vamp-pallor thing you usually rock."

Leaning closer to the tiny mirror to examine the light smattering of freckles that appeared across my nose, I frown. Then I school my expression once I see how deep those frown lines are. "Is it really that bad?"

Renna is at my side in an instant, and I know she heard the true worry in my voice.

"Oh, honey, no. You're stunning. You've always been stunning. It's just I never had anything to compare it to, and now that I've seen how healthy and happy you look with a little sun and relaxation, I can't help but notice, well, you…"

She trails off, and I snap the compact shut and power off my laptop.

"Maybe I'll order a new bronzer." I double-check my purse to ensure it's packed for every possible emergency, then give her a quick hug on my way out the door. "I'll text you if I find anything interesting at the charity auction."

My phone pings as I step into the elevator, letting me know my driver has arrived.

And I am, once again, an impenetrable force of stoic strength.

My hands are no longer sweating. The knots in my

stomach have untangled. I'm doing what I love to do, the way I love to do it. My business is running smoothly, my clients are happy, and my employees are valued. Every *i* has been dotted, every *t* has been crossed. I've returned to my perfect state of equilibrium now that I've made the informed decision to separate my personal life from my work, and I've never felt better.

Glancing at the time as I duck into my waiting car, I smile and congratulate myself for my composure and control because I've made it three minutes past my two-hour text-back rule.

****

Malcolm

I read over Ryan's message and check the timestamp.

2:34 —I'm off to a charity auction, then attending a seminar on the impacts of social media trends on digital marketing.—

As frustrated as I am with her sudden return to formalities and arm's-length communication, I can't help but find it weirdly cute she's obviously adhering to some two-hour rule when it comes to replying to me.

My date for the afternoon is Callianne, a woman old enough to be my great-grandmother, and I have to admit I'm having a blast escorting her through the shops on Rodeo Drive. Playing the role of a pack mule has been made infinitely more enjoyable by her insistence we stop to people-watch every thirty minutes. I introduced her to my backstory game, and there's a chance I created a monster, but I'm not going to complain, not when her imagination is so damn good.

"That young man over there is a world-renowned thumb wrestler," she tells me, pointing to a guy fifteen years my senior. "He sank his fortune into glass-bottom trains and now lives in his mother's ex-husband's uncle's basement, making cuss-word needlepoint he sells online." She grins at me and pats my leg. "Was that your honey who messaged you?"

I wince because I know better than to check my phone during work hours. "Sorry. Yeah, kind of? I think? Maybe?"

Calianne gives me a look that makes my balls shrivel and retreat in fear. "You think, kind of, maybe? Malcolm, my dear. It wasn't that hard a question."

"It is where Ryan is concerned." I grunt, shoving a hand through my hair. "I like her. I think she likes me, too, but things are complicated."

"Ah," she hums. "She's married."

Scoffing, I shake my head and laugh. "What? No, she's not married."

"Then she lives in another state," she says knowingly. "A long-distance relationship."

I shake my head.

Her eyes widen. "She's pregnant with another man's child."

"No!" I choke out, the mere thought of Ryan allowing any other man to touch her boiling my blood. "Jeez, Callianne. Are you trying to give me a heart attack?"

Her frail arms cross. "If it's not marriage, distance, or another man's baby in her belly, what else could possibly be so complicated you don't know if the woman who makes you smile at your phone like a damn fool is your honey?"

I open my mouth to explain, but snap it shut when I realized she's on to something.

Not seeing her for the last two weeks has sucked despite how strong my surf game has been and how padded my bank account is getting. These timed text responses are just enough to keep me checking my phone in some Pavlovian response but nowhere near enough to sate me.

I. Want. Ryan.

I want to see her bite her lip when she needs a moment to think. I want her perfectly grammatical texts pinging my phone all night. I want to hear her voice before I go to bed. I want to experience that rush of anticipation I feel every time I know she's moments away from stepping onto my beach.

And as much as I might tease her about her lists and her calendar and her color-coded schedules, I want to be on those lists and calendars and schedules. I want her phone to chime with an alert reminding her we have a date. I want to see my name in a blue color block. I want more of those moments when we go offtrack and she steadies her breath, steeling herself for the change before trusting me and jumping in.

I want her on the board beside me.

Calianne pats my knee. "I think we're done here, my dear. Why don't you help my driver load those bags into the trunk and go figure out if you have a honey?"

Frowning, I check the time. "We still have an hour."

"Go," she huffs, the gentle pat become a swat on my thigh strong enough to make me flinch. "My back hurts, and I'm ready to put my feet up. We'll hit the other side of the street next time, sweet boy."

I collect the shopping bags piled around us, arrange them in the trunk, and help her into the car. "You're a saint, Calianne."

"And you're a fool if you don't go after your maybe-honey right now."

On that note, she drives away with a wave, and I wander over to my truck, flipping my phone between my fingers.

Even with this date ending early, the shift in my bookings means there still isn't enough time for me to head home between dates. My suit is hanging on the passenger side, my polished shoes tucked inside a bag to keep them spotless until tonight. I have a jar of hair product in my glovebox in case I need it and a near-empty bottle of cologne sitting in the cup holder.

If only I had somewhere to hang out for an hour or two. Someone to hang out with.

Drumming my fingers on the steering wheel, I debate how creepy I want to get here.

I could text her my standard *hey, how are you.*

I could call and leave a message she won't listen to.

Or I could go along with the questionably insistent thought looping through my mind.

Decision made, I rev the engine and turn onto the street.

I may not know where she works, but I know the neighborhood. And it happens to be close to Doll Parts, giving me a half-decent alibi should I be lucky enough to run into her.

My music is cranked up on the drive, providing a good distraction from the knowledge I'm officially half-assed stalking Ryan. I manage to assuage enough of my guilt to park and get out, but not enough to keep my shoulders from tensing or my palms from going clammy.

I'm one block into my creeper stroll when I come to the harsh realization this is weird. Pointless. Every office building in the vicinity is designed for privacy, every window tinted or mirrored or shuttered. Signage is discreet, and employees are hidden from view. Figuring it's karma's way of telling me to back the hell off, I decide to circle back past Doll Parts on my way to my truck. I'm digging a decent well to pour my self-pity into when a car pulls to a stop alongside me and the back door swings open, narrowly missing me.

Armed with a withering glare, I prepare to give the guy a stare down to end all stare downs when the profile of a woman I'd know anywhere comes into view. "Ryan?"

Chapter Twelve

Ryan

My accountant's voice continues to blather through my earpiece a mile a minute while I remain frozen in place, one foot on the curb, and the other still inside the car. A faint breeze slips up my skirt and skims along my exposed thigh, making me hyperaware of just how much I'm channeling CEO-chic today.

"Malcolm." I hang up on Brody without warning. I can't listen to shareholder reports while my mind is spinning to meld my Malcolm world with my real one. "What are you doing here?"

He runs a hand through his hair, and my own fingers ache to do it for him.

He looks so. Damn. Good.

"I was in the neighborhood," he says, shrugging like he often does when he's uncomfortable. "Decided to take a walk."

I fully exit the car and give my driver what I hope is a polite smile and wave, refusing to look at the Doll Parts sign hanging above the door behind him in case he hasn't realized where he is. "It's, um, good to see you."

I feel naked right now. Naked and exposed with a huge L for Liar painted on my forehead. My heart is pounding hard enough to break a rib, and for once it isn't because Malcolm looks so deliciously bitable.

My secret is right there.

Right. There.

One turn of his head and he'll see it. He'll see it, put two and two together, and—

"I lied," he blurts out, closing the distance between us. "I know you work somewhere around here, so I figured I'd make the excuse of being in the area in the hopes I'd run into you."

I take a deep, relieved breath, and his expression shifts into one of sheepishness.

"I know." Both hands are now pushing through that glorious mane of his. "It's a total creeper move, using Doll Parts as an excuse to be here. But I wanted to see you, and you weren't answering my calls, and you were doing that whole text-timing-response thing so—" He gives me a tight smile. "So I channeled my inner nut job, and while I feel bad about coming around under false pretenses, I'm not really regretting it right now because hi."

My laugh is an inelegant bark I know I'll relive a dozen times before midnight. "Well then, hi to you, too."

When his dimple appears and his blue eyes light up, I struggle to remember why it was I thought keeping him at arm's length was a good plan. Because I much prefer him in touching distance.

We must be riding the same wavelength because he takes my hand, places my palm on his chest, and traces my fingers with his thumb. "Do you have time to grab a coffee? I saw a mobile truck down the street advertising the best lattes in the county."

I can't help but glance up over his shoulder toward the window behind Renna's desk. The shade is drawn, but no way am I going to tempt fate any longer than I have to. "Yes, I think I do. Follow me."

He doesn't put up a fight when I grab his hand and all but drag him down the block as fast as my four-inch heels will allow. Paranoia kicks in, and I swear I can hear my lying soul sigh in disappointment because I'm a fugitive on the run. A fugitive who was due to meet her best friend for a scheduling review five minutes ago. Any second now, my phone will buzz, and I'll either have to ignore it or reply with another little fib, another tiny detail in the web I keep spinning.

But Malcolm's hand feels so right clutching mine. We walk in sync. We breathe in sync. Coming clean in this moment when he looks so happy to be with me would be cruel.

"So which office is yours?" he asks as he approaches the order counter and scans the glass towers surrounding us.

I place my request for the best damn latte in the county and smile at him. "All of them. A big part of my job involves discovering holes needing filled and filling those holes with top talent."

The lie rolls off my tongue with such ease I scare myself.

I am not a liar.

At least, I never used to be.

He tilts his head, and his brows knot. "Like a headhunter?"

"Exactly like a headhunter."

Technically, I am very much a headhunter. I search for gaps in the lives of my clients and ensure Doll Parts is equipped to smooth those gaps over. And while "all of them" may have been a bit of an exaggeration when he asked which office is mine, I do own my building and one farther down the block that I rent out to a dozen startup enterprises for competitive prices.

But no amount of rationalization can make my words honest. I have to tell him the truth. I know I do.

He gives me a lopsided grin and shakes his head. "So my woman is even more badass than I thought."

"Your woman?"

"Yup."

His confidence should make me balk as I always envisioned I would do with such a declaration.

Except I don't because I want to be his. And I want him to be mine.

I want him to look at me like this every day, with that mischievous glint and damn dimple. I want his hand around mine just like it is now, guiding me toward a wrought iron bench where we can sip our lattes and talk about nothing important.

Once he learns I'm not who he thinks I am, I know I'll lose all this, and I'm not ready. My attempt to distance myself physically from him did nothing to severe the emotional connection I've got to this man. The last two weeks have been an exercise in torturous restraint and deceitful self-talk.

I am not a pillar of strength when it comes to Malcolm. I'm mush. Lying, deceitful mush.

"So did you do some hiring work with Doll Parts?"

Snapping out of my stare down with my coffee, I force a smile and tell a half-truth. "Actually, yes, I did."

He nods. "You must be the genius behind Renna Merchant, then. She's the woman who does the hiring and scheduling over there. She's very cool. I like her."

"She likes you, too," I say without thinking, my eyes widening when I hear my own words.

"Oh yeah?" His voice is light and teasing. "Did she recommend me to you? If so, I'm sending her flowers."

Heat burns my cheeks, and I stand and brush nonexistent dust from my thighs. "She said I would adore you."

He gets up and takes my empty coffee cup from my hand before tossing it in the trash and flashing me a charming grin. "And?"

Biting my lip, I shrug like seeing him hasn't made me happier than I've been in two weeks. "She wasn't wrong."

****

Malcolm

With my phone tight to my ear, I stand close to the edge of my rooftop escape and watch the reflection of the moon ripple across the waves. "Then I'll come to you."

Ryan's laugh is quiet, and I can picture her sitting in the back of a black SUV with her eyes closed after a long evening. "It's midnight."

"It's been five days since I've seen you. What's your address?"

"I'm already on the move."

The smile in her voice tells me I've won the long-fought battle to see her tonight.

"I'll be there in fifteen minutes," she continues. "But I'm not staying long."

Ignoring her addendum, I head down to check the state of my apartment and grab my keys. "Have your driver drop you off at the usual corner, and I'll meet you there. I don't want you walking alone."

"I'll be fine."

"And I'm not arguing," I say, heading out the door

and taking the steps two at a time. "How did it go today?"

She sighs, and I pick up my pace, eager to be there when she arrives so she can lean on me.

"I'm cross-eyed from staring at my computer screen for seventeen hours, my tailbone is aching from the flights, I'm jittery from eating chocolate-covered coffee beans, and apparently whining is my newest coping mechanism."

"Whine away, baby. I want to hear it all."

And I do.

Hours after our impromptu latte date, Ryan texted me to let me know she would be MIA for a bit. Two days later, she called from Michigan. The next morning, she sent me a text letting me know she was fine and with her mother.

I didn't buy into the whole "fine" thing then, and I don't now.

I stand on the corner and listen to her vent about the connecting flights she had to take, her frustration with the meetings she needed to reschedule, and the poor internet connection at the motel where she was holed up. I wait for her to mention her mom, but it never comes, and my need to see her and wrap my arms around her grows with every hoarse word she speaks.

I may not know what happened in Michigan yet, but I do know this is the first time she's sounded defeated, and it's killing me.

"Is that you standing under the streetlight?" she asks.

I wave at the black SUV stopped at a red light up the block. "You bet."

She exhales loudly. "You might want to run away now. I'm pretty cranky."

Scoffing, I approach the car as it slows to a stop. "I don't run."

I open the passenger door, hang up our call, and hold out my hand to her. The smile she gives me when she stands seems to take the last of her energy, and she wobbles on her high heels. Her eyes dart behind me to the smattering of people milling around the few open restaurants, and her shoulders square with effort as a hardened resolve settles in her tired eyes.

I want to pick her up and carry her home, but I've seen this look on her face before. She needs to project an aura of control no matter how exhausted or upset she is.

And now that she's here with me, I can see how much she didn't say during our intermittent phone calls over the last five days. I take her large bag and purse off her shoulder and grasp her hand in silence, trying not to let my internal freak-out show on my face as I study her.

Her eyes are red-rimmed and vacant, bordering on full zombie. She's pale, and I can feel a slight tremble where her cold palm touches mine. Every step is measured and weighted, as though she's counting them down to keep herself going. Her breathing is shallow with a slight rasp on each sharp inhale.

We reach the stairs, and her lips purse.

"What are the chances you'll let me carry you up?" I ask, adjusting her bags on my shoulder in the off chance she lets me.

"Zero."

I let her lead the way, keeping one hand inches from her back in case she stumbles and breathing out a sigh of relief when she makes it to the top without collapsing.

Wrapping one arm around her waist, I open the door and guide her straight to the sofa. "Don't move."

I set her bags on the bathroom counter and turn the shower on to let it heat up.

My shower is awesome, for lack of a better word. Saltwater and sand are my life, so I invest heavily in ways to wash it away. Between the oversized rain showerhead and the strong spray of the detachable handheld, standing in the large tiled space is akin to heaven.

I add two fresh towels, one of my tees, and a pair of sweatpants to her pile before I return to the living room to find her exactly where I left her, shoes still on and her spine ramrod straight. I kneel down and slide her heels off, surprised when she doesn't protest.

"I'm going to get a midnight snack together while you rinse off and get warm," I order, helping her to her feet. "Take as long as you need. I have one of those tankless heating systems."

She still doesn't argue, and I don't like it. My air conditioning has made the apartment comfortably cool, but her fingers are ice. The only indication she's still inside this zombie is the side-eye she gives me as she steps into the bathroom and looks around.

"This is prettier than I remembered."

With that, the door closes, and I head to the kitchen to raid my fridge and cupboards to assemble a decent spread. I keep one ear open to her movements, pleased when I catch a change in the sound of the water but ready to bust in if I hear anything resembling a fall.

Ten minutes pass. Then fifteen. At twenty, I have my ear pressed to the door, torn between calling out to check in with her and leaving her alone. By the time the water turns off, I'm pacing the hall with my phone in hand, waiting for the faint movements I can make out to stop and ready to call 9-1-1 in a heartbeat.

I know I'm bordering on some super creeper behavior as I remain in the hall and listen to the sound of her riffling through her bags, but I can't stop myself. This version of Ryan freaks me out, this woman moving on autopilot. My imagination is whipping up all sorts of horrific scenarios to account for it, jumping from the reasonable explanation of her being stressed and tired to the likelihood she's been assaulted or threatened.

I don't remember feeling like this with any other woman. Protective and concerned, sure, but not this rabid, baseless fear. I've seen Ryan when she's out of her element, when she's off-kilter, when she's upset, and when she's annoyed, but she always radiates a certain self-assuredness as her beautiful mind organizes and adapts to whatever is going on.

But this? She looks lost. Lost and defeated.

And I recognize that look because I wore it for months after my injury.

I'm on high alert when she finally emerges from the bathroom in a cloud of steam. Her wet hair is brushed long and smooth, dampening my blue shirt, which is practically drowning her. My sweatpants hang low on her hips, the drawstring dangling in a long bow. The dark circles under her eyes are more pronounced now that her face is scrubbed clean, and I can make out a smattering of freckles across the bridge of her nose.

"This looks good," she murmurs as she sits on the sofa in front of the charcuterie I managed to assemble. "Thank you."

I open a bottle of water, pass it over, and sit beside her. "My pleasure. What else do you need?"

She has to need something. She's still too stilted, too

robotic. And whatever it is she names, I'm ready and willing to do or find or buy.

"Distraction," she replies, picking at a cheese slice.

I grab the television remote, put on a tried-and-true superhero flick without a word, and pretend to watch alongside her until she curls into a ball and falls into a dead sleep.

Chapter Thirteen

Ryan

Before I even open my eyes, I know I'm not in my penthouse, and I'm definitely not in a motel in the middle of Buttfuck, Michigan. The blanket is a perfect balance of weighted without smothering. The pillow under my head is softer than what I prefer, but it smells like a combination of fresh linen with a hint of lavender, and I want to burrow deeper into this nest I'm in and hide forever.

"Good morning, Sleeping Beauty."

In a move pro wrestlers would be impressed with, I spin and flip out of my blanket cocoon to land on my knees in the middle of the bed, ready to defend myself against—

"Malcolm?" I blink as he stands in the doorway and grips the top of the frame, the motion inching his shirt above the band of his board shorts and giving me a peek of his V-cut. "What are you doing here?"

Concern darkens his blue eyes, and his biceps tighten as he holds his position. "What do you remember about last night?"

Last night.

Last night.

Last night, my plane touched down after three connecting flights and a three-hour layover in Houston.

My driver picked me up, and I powered on my phone, my stomach knotting when my text and email notifications pinged in rapid succession. I remember feeling like I was drowning, like I couldn't swim fast enough to stay afloat.

All I could think about was that the five days I spent dealing with the fallout of my mother's latest failed engagement managed to topple my carefully constructed calendar and schedule for the year. Meetings would need to be rebooked. Paperwork was piling up. Calls, texts, and emails needed to be returned. All of it had to be done yesterday.

I sat in the back of the SUV, frozen in terror when I realized my brain was broken. I couldn't find a beginning. I couldn't think of where to start. My notifications seemed to increase exponentially, growing and twisting into a rope anchoring me in place and keeping me immobile.

And so I called him.

I remember the overpowering need to hear his voice. Just his voice. I didn't need to see him or touch him. I simply needed him to ground me for a minute, to be the calm to balance the chaos in my mind.

Looking around the room, I realize I'm in his bed. In his bedroom. I recognize the plaid pattern on the blanket and the exposed beams crossing the ceiling. I catch my reflection in his dresser mirror, and my brows shoot up at the sight of what I'm wearing and the state of my hair. "Did we…"

With a look I can only describe as horror, he shakes his head, and his damp hair slaps off his shoulders. "God no. No. I wouldn't… You… We didn't…" He shoves a hand through his hair. "No."

Insulted, I sit back on my haunches. "Okay, I get it."

He's visibly cringing as he releases the doorframe and takes a step into the room. "I mean, I want to. I would. God, would I ever. But not when—" Exhaling loudly, he crosses his arms. "How are you feeling?"

Good question.

Snippets of the night before are filtering into my mind now that I'm fully awake. The relief I felt when I saw him standing under the streetlamp. The walk here. The shower. The sensation of his fingers raking through my hair and caressing my forehead.

My cheeks burn with embarrassment as I recall pleading with him to stay with me when he carried me to bed.

Covering my face with my hands, I drop my head forward and squeeze my eyes shut.

I am strength. I am power. I am unstoppable.

I am also clingy and whiny and a hot mess sitting on Malcolm's bed while he watches me have a mini breakdown.

"Ryan?"

The mattress dips as I take a deep breath, find my center, and regain my control. Smoothing my hair back, I sit up and give him the most genuine smile I can summon. "I'm good. All good. Good."

His lips quirk up. "So you're good?"

"Yes. All good."

"All, hey?"

I realize he's teasing me and give him my best don't-even-think-about-starting-it stare. "Malcolm."

He reaches over and takes my hand, lacing his fingers through mine. "You have no idea how happy I am to see that look on your face right now." Letting me go, he stands and flashes me that dimpled smile, which makes my heart flutter. "Breakfast is ready, so come out as soon as you're ready."

I watch him walk out of the room, my eyes drawn to the way his board shorts cling to his ass. Like his hair, they're damp and accenting every muscle of his finely tuned backside, and I realize the smell of the ocean is fading the longer he's gone from the room, which means he's already been out on the water this morning.

And if he's already been out on the water—

With my head doing a full-on *Exorcist* spin in my desperate hunt for a clock, I scramble off the bed and fling the blanket and pillow onto the floor, searching for my phone before remembering the last time I saw my purse, it was on the bathroom counter.

I tear out of the bedroom and find my travel carry-on but no purse.

No purse.

No purse and no phone.

"Malcolm?" I call out, my panic evident in the high pitch of my voice. "Have you seen my purse?"

"It's out here in the kitchen. Want me to bring it to you?"

Relieved, I take a deep breath and catch my reflection in the mirror, coming to a screeching halt. "No." I lean in closer to examine my appearance. "No thank you."

I look every bit as stressed and agitated as I'm feeling. My eyes and hair are wild, my skin pale with a fevered flush on my cheeks. I have no disguise to hide behind without makeup, a curling iron, and a designer wardrobe. I have no barrier to block anyone from seeing me for the disaster I've been since I arrived in Michigan to find my mother groveling—groveling on her hands and knees—on the doorstep of her ex-fiancé's townhouse.

I ease the door closed, open my carry-on, empty it onto the counter, and do my best to assemble what little armor I can with the few essentials I never fly without.

Toothbrush. Toothpaste. Brush. Lip gloss. Clear nail polish. Two pairs of stockings. One pair of black ballet flats.

I forgo the shoes and stockings, but after brushing my teeth and hair and praising my own forethought to stock up on tinted lip gloss, I feel almost human. Or at least human enough to face the gorgeous man making me breakfast.

The gorgeous man who will probably have some questions about the state I was in last night.

Squaring my shoulders, I exit the bathroom, walk into the kitchen, and stop in the entranceway to watch him.

I've never been good in the kitchen, and I've never cared if anyone else was, but seeing him slide the sunny-side eggs onto two plates already loaded with hash browns, bacon, and toast does something to me.

With the practiced flip of his wrist, he turns off the stove and sets the plates on the table where two cups of coffee and two glasses of orange juice are already set out.

It's so…domestic.

"Hungry?"

Ripped from my stare down with the carefully laid-out cutlery, I nod. "Starving. Thank you."

I'm out of my element as I sit and fidget with my napkin. There are no waiters, delivery drivers, or explicit microwave instructions detailed on the top of the cardboard packaging. There's no discussion agenda or the expectation to finalize details before lawyers take over. It's just us.

"The weather is supposed to take a real turn again later this afternoon," he says as he takes the seat across from me and digs right in. "It kind of sucks we won't be able to hit the water later, but at least it's the perfect excuse for us to hole up and do nothing."

My fork pauses an inch from my lips. "Us?"

He starts laying out a list of movie franchises we could binge-watch, then stops and looks pointedly at my uneaten food. "Are your eggs okay?"

Blinking, I look down at my plate, then at him. "Perfect. But I'm sorry. I can't spend the day here. I have to get to the office and start dealing with—"

"It's your day off," he interjects, nodding in the direction of my purse. "Your boss said so."

My boss?

My fork clatters on the plate as I jump up, grab my phone from my purse, and scan the litany of messages lighting it up.

Malcolm's hand covers the screen immediately. "You can check those after you eat a few more bites. The two crackers and three slices of cheese you ate last night aren't enough."

When I open my mouth to protest, he ducks his head down and kisses me, silencing me with his lips and tongue until the death grip I've had on my phone relaxes, and he eases it back into my purse.

"Fine," I mutter when he smiles against my mouth. "A few bites. But then I need to get moving. It's already late."

Apparently satisfied with my answer, he leads me

back to the table and sits. "It's only noon."

I'm on my feet in a heartbeat, and I can feel tension building along my spine as I think about the monumental buildup of missed meetings and appointments. "Noon?"

This time, he isn't as sweet when he stands and nudges me back into my chair. "Eat. You're pale and shaking, and frankly, it's really starting to freak me out here, Ryan."

We enter a silent power struggle, him tanned and strong and staring me down with every slice of bacon he inhales, and me with my fork feeling heavy in my weary, worried hand.

With my calendar loading inside my head, I take a bite of the eggs. Mentally reshuffling my schedule again, I take another. Bite by bite, I try to recall every color-coded time block and shrink each by ten minutes here, fifteen minutes there.

When most of my breakfast is eaten, he pushes his empty plate aside, leans back in his chair, and crosses his arms. "Now how do you feel?"

"I—" I pause and frown. I'm stressed and anxious and wondering who exactly he believes my boss is, but underneath it all— "I feel a bit better."

His grin isn't cocky. If anything, he looks like he was given a gold star for a job well done as he clears our plates and grabs my phone from my purse for me. "Good. Now check your messages from Big Bad Boss Bitch and see for yourself that you have the day off."

I pull up Renna's texts immediately, grateful for the nickname I assigned her last year during a particularly hectic Christmas season when she literally broke out a whip and hung it behind my desk as a reminder to adhere to her meticulously constructed schedule.

—Your quarterly meet with Peters starts in fifteen. Where are you?—

—I need time to recuperate. Can you cover?—

—About damn time you took a day. I'll sit in and clear your calendar. Make it a real hooky day. Go find a stallion to ride for a few hours, and I'll empty tomorrow's schedule for you, too.—

Malcolm read the whole exchange, and the realization makes my cheeks flame up. I zero in on the message sent by me while I was still sound asleep in his bed. "Did you pretend to be me?"

He has the gall to shrug and nod as he rinses the dishes and loads them into the dishwasher. "I saw her text ping in while I was on my way out to catch the morning waves. You were out cold and exhausted, and it's obvious even your boss knows you need to take a break."

Shaking my head in disbelief, I lean on the counter and meet his gaze. "You can't do that. I needed to be in that meeting."

"Did you?"

"I—"

Thinking about the quarterly rundowns I've been sitting through with my building manager Wendall Peters for the last eight years, I try to recall a single piece of information he's shared over time that couldn't have been in an email.

I built my reputation on being a personal touch and a human connection, putting myself front and center so no one could forget who made decisions about Doll Parts, my real estate holdings, and my tech investments. I did it to be the recognizable face of the company while we grew from the ground up, giving the only thing I could afford in the beginning—my time.

Except my time had value. Value I forgot it carried.

"No, I guess I didn't," I say slowly, sinking onto one of the barstools lining the countertop and bringing up my calendar, shocked by the empty blocks filling the screen. "I don't actually need to be anywhere right now. Or doing anything."

He starts the dishwasher, rounds the counter, and his arms come around me moments before he kisses the top of my head. "Sure you do. You need to get on the couch and pick the franchise we're binge-watching."

****

Malcolm

Eighteen months ago, the best Friday nights were spent at the club with my surf crew, a beer in my hand and a decent shot of winning a few rounds of pool while my wife was out with her more palatable crew and my credit card. Sometimes the club was replaced by a bonfire on the beach or a house party, but the beer and the company stayed the same.

Tonight, with Ryan curled up beside me on my sofa, blows every other Friday night away. A half-eaten pizza is sitting on the coffee table. She's rustling a bag of chips and asking a million questions about the storylines, characters, and actors in the movies we've been watching for eight hours straight, aside from a brief pause for her to have a quick shower and dress in another one of my shirts-and-sweats combos. Stillness is not her forte. Neither is regulating her body temperature, judging by the number of times she's burrowed under the blanket she took from my bed only to toss it off twenty minutes later.

And I'm in heaven.

This right here? With her tucked under my arm while she crinkles the foil bag a few more times? This is where I want to be every night from here on out.

We haven't spoken a word about last night or her job. Neither of us has mentioned me putting her phone on the top shelf of the hall closet. She hasn't asked why I'm not working, and I haven't asked when she has to leave. Keeping her out of her head is my only goal. She isn't putting up a fight.

The closing credits on the fifth film roll, and I cue up the next one. We're existing in a delicate bubble, and I'm not letting a lull in our superhero watch-fest burst it anytime soon.

An intense action sequence opens the sixth movie, and she shifts position again, scooting out from under my arm. Before I can object, she grabs a throw cushion, sets it on my lap, and lies down.

My protest dies on my tongue.

Call me a jerk, but as much as I'm loving having this relaxed, chill version of Ryan, I can't shake the memory of her boss's text all but demanding she find a stallion to ride.

The thought of Ryan taking any other man for a spin isn't one I'm willing to entertain because if I do, there's a good chance I'll resort to some illegal caveman bullshit, which would not only send Ryan running for the hills but probably get me arrested in the process.

She fights the blanket off her shoulders for the hundredth time and settles again, one hand now resting on my thigh. My cock reacts before my brain can, and I hope she didn't feel the twitch through the pillow.

"I don't remember ever seeing my mom do this with any of her boyfriends or husbands," she says softly.

"Maybe that's her mistake. She never slows down long enough to just exist with someone."

All thought of where her fingers are evaporates. I can't claim I've been an open book with her given the bullshit drama with my dad and my ex, but getting anything personal out of Ryan has been an uphill battle since the beginning.

I lay my hand on her hip and still. If she's talking now, I'm shutting up and giving her the floor. She continues after a long pause, her attention on the television.

"My mom loves to be in love. All my life, there's been this revolving door of losers she swore would be The One but who eventually left her more broke and more broken than ever. We moved in with seventeen of them while I was growing up, sometimes in the same city but not always." She shifts, her knees drawing up to her chest like she's protecting it. "Right before my high school grad, she actually managed to scrape together enough money to put a downpayment on a beaten-up bungalow. It was heaven, living in a home we couldn't be kicked out of when some man got fed up with her. But that May she met an old guy who swooped in and moved her to Brazil. My mom sold our old house and left a note reminding me I needed to be out by the fifteenth of July. My scholarship to the University of Southern California didn't kick in until September, so I couch-surfed for six weeks." Tilting her head up, she looks at me and gives me a wry smile. "That marriage lasted seven months, three months longer than the one during my sophomore year."

Pieces of Ryan's puzzle slide into place: her need for control, her aversion to dating, the careful scheduling, and need to plan. Growing up at the whim of a mother who changed boyfriends more than most people changed their furnace filters had to have an impact on her.

A disturbing thought came into my head.

"These guys," I open slowly, not certain it's my place to brooch the subject. "Were any of them…too friendly?"

She shivers. "No. I was lucky my mom seemed to have a sixth sense about creeps. Her Loser Radar was damaged as hell, but she never brought around any men who showed any interest in me. Ever." Scoffing, she turns back to the television. "I was shocked whenever one remembered to put a plate out for me at dinner."

Relief floods me, but it's countered by the image I conjure of a young Ryan sitting along in a dark apartment, invisible and unwanted. The urge to wrap my arms around her and promise her she'll never be unseen, unheard, or unwanted again surges in my chest, and I know without a doubt I've fallen harder than I've ever fallen before or ever will again.

The hand on my thigh wraps a little tighter, almost hugging me as she sighs. "This time I got a text from her telling me she needed money to win her man back. She wouldn't respond to my messages, so I hopped a flight to Michigan and went to the last address she'd given me." Her voice becomes flat, emotionless. "I found her on her hands and knees clawing at her ex's front door and begging him to love her. The only way I could get her out of there was to promise I would pay for a makeover her ex-fiancé couldn't resist."

"Did it work?"

She rolls onto her back, and her blue eyes lock with

mine. "No. Not on Tony, anyways. I spent the next four days bouncing between hairdressers and nail salons and malls while my mother wailed and collapsed on every soft surface we came across." She pushes a stray strand of hair off her face. "I had to find her a furnished apartment she could move into immediately, set up her bills under my name thanks to a fiancé she had four years ago who obliterated her credit score, and convince Tony not to press charges when she broke into his house through a window in the middle of the night."

Whistling low, I shake my head, despising what her mother put her through but loving the fact she's sharing it with me. "No wonder you were such a zombie last night."

"Oh, that wasn't the best part," she states, tugging the blanket up under her chin. "Three hours before I flew out, I asked her to walk over to a pizza joint up the way and grab dinner. She came home with two pepperoni pizzas and a new soul mate."

I can't stop the drop of my jaw. "No."

"Yup. The bassist for Tony's 'we're going to make it big someday' cover band. He needed a place to live because his ex-wife kicked him out of the garage where he's been living for the past three years, and my mom decided fate brought them together to live in eternal bliss. I lost five days of work I'll have to make up somehow in my already insane schedule, spent a king's ransom to set her up for success, and all it took was a greasy bass player with no talent and no job to remind me why I'll never fall in love."

I blink.

Well, shit.

Chapter Fourteen

Ryan

I've heard decent things about scream therapy. I even considered it a few years back when Doll Parts was big enough to turn a profit and not large enough to be stable. But the cathartic process of screaming into the void couldn't possibly compete with how I'm feeling now, lying on Malcolm's sofa with my head in his lap after purging about my mother.

No one knows how tough the end of my mom's relationships can be. They hear "breakup" and think a few nights of ice cream and crying peppered with proclamations of moving on, moving up, and moving out. And I've never tried to explain, not even to Renna and Brit. Nobody needs to know how many times I've been called to pick her up from the police station for public intoxication, trespassing, or mischief. They don't need to hear about the three a.m. wailing phone calls or the hours I've spent driving through unfamiliar cities searching for her before she tracks down her latest ex's new love interest and makes a scene. It's not something I share with anyone, ever.

Knowing I blathered on to Malcolm has me disoriented, but in the best way. I feel a little freer. A little lighter. The secret is out, and he hasn't looked at me with pity or revulsion or made a joke about psycho ex-girlfriends. Better yet, he hasn't shuffled away from me like I've caught my mother's lovesickness and might turn it onto him. His hand is still resting on my hip, and his fingers are tracing small circles over the shirt he handed me without hesitation when I announced I wanted a quick shower before I got comfortable again.

And I am comfortable. Maybe too comfortable. The outside world doesn't exist right now, and I'm not sorry to be missing it.

But I am a little sorry I unloaded on him.

Burrowing my face into his muscled stomach, I sigh. "Thanks for letting me vent. And for keeping the whole pity thing in check."

"Families kind of suck, don't they?" he says, his hand squeezing my hipbone gently. "My dad is the guy I'm bidding against for this apartment and the store."

I sit up and face him, scooting closer on my knees. "No. Why? Why would he do that?"

He chuckles and runs a hand through his hair. "Long story short, he blames me for destroying his pro career and decided a while back that I owed him mine."

Frowning, I grab the remote and pause the movie. "Doesn't he realize what it means to you?"

"He knows exactly what it means to me." He sighs, drumming his fingers on the armrest of the sofa. "The way he sees it, I was bad luck for him since the day I was born. He was rising to the top of the circuit, racking up sponsors, and traveling the world when my mom got pregnant. I arrived on the scene, and everything went to hell. He couldn't hold a wave, lost his deals, and my mom walked out on us, all in the first three years."

His voice is flat and unaffected, but I can see the resentment in his eyes, and I can't resist wrapping my arms around him as he continues.

"When I was younger, I thought he might be on to something because nothing ever seemed to go right for us. But the longer I worked the waves, the more stories I heard about his drinking and partying and how he was this prodigy who managed to fuck himself over because his ego was stronger than his discipline." His arms tighten around me, and he rests his cheek on the top of my head. "Buying Barreled is his way of getting that last piece of what I worked for. I guess he figures if he can muscle me out of the last thing tying me to the water, he wins or something."

"He doesn't know you're trying for a comeback, does he?" I ask, my mind shifting into business gear as the urge to step between Malcolm and his father swells. "How far would he go to sabotage you?"

"As far as he had to." He shifts beneath me, and I look up to see him glaring at the frozen television screen. "There's a good chance he knows. Or suspects. It's not like the beach is private, and we still have a lot of overlap in our contacts, so…" Trailing off, he shrugs. "As long as I keep working as much as I have been lately, I should win the blind bid for the property."

A thought pops into my head, and I speak before I think. "I could help you."

His eyes harden. "I'm not taking money from my girlfriend."

"It's not taking money from your girlfriend," I huff, secretly thrilled with the label but outwardly annoyed at his tone. "Call it a loan. A Fuck-You loan if you want."

Shoving his hand through his hair, he exhales loudly. "I'm not discussing this. No. Mixing business and pleasure is a guaranteed disaster." Returning his hand to my hip, he relaxes. "I appreciate the offer, but I need to do this alone. If my dad found out you were involved, he would make your life hell. Or worse."

I can't help but think about my mom. She's imperfect and unpredictable and unreliable, and no one could ever accuse her of putting her child above all else, but I never felt like she didn't love me in her own way. She did. She loved me fiercely because that's the only way my mom knows how to love. It's the reason I would forever be there with every heartbreak.

Compared to Malcolm's dad going out of his way to ruin his son's future, my mom borders on award-worthy.

I straddle his hips and run my thumb along his scruffy jaw. "Your dad is an asshole, and if you want me to beat him up, I will. I've survived hot yoga. I can kick a former surfer's ass any day."

His gaze drops to my mouth as he licks his lips. "I'll keep that in mind if I lose the bid. Which I won't."

He thinks I'm joking, but a seed has been planted. Before he can see the cogs in my mind churning, I close the gap between us and kiss him.

Kissing Malcolm is unlike any other lip-lock I've ever experienced. He's the perfect balance of sensual and playful, demanding and gentle. He nips and licks before easing into feathery brushes that skim my lips and throat. His hunger for me is tangible, an aphrodisiac that makes me hot, needy, and unbalanced.

Linking my fingers with his, I stand, and he follows, his lips never leaving mine as I tug him toward his bedroom. I'm unsteady and a little unsure, not knowing how bold I should be but not willing to wait any longer, because I no longer want him. I need him. I need his hands and his mouth and the low groans I hear when we stumble into his room, and he presses me up against the wall.

"I love seeing you in my clothes," he growls, grabbing the hem of my shirt and pulling it over my head. His eyes darken, and he swallows as he grazes his fingers along the lace trim of my cobalt-blue bra. "But I definitely love this view more."

He takes a step back and hooks his thumbs in the band of the basketball shorts hanging low on my hips. He kneels as he lowers them to the floor, and I'm hit with a wave of self-consciousness.

I know I look good in my matching bra and lacy boy shorts, but it's thirty-six-year-old good, and I can't help but wonder what he sees in this moment. His hands are splayed on my hips as he takes in every inch of me, and I go still, studying him while he memorizes me.

"Fuck." He finally breathes out, his fingers digging into my skin. "You really are going to ruin me, aren't you?"

****

Malcolm

I can't move because if I do I'm either going to maul Ryan or come in my board shorts. Neither is optimal. I'm on my knees before a goddess, and the reality of this moment has already surpassed every fantasy I've had since the night I met this woman. She has curves and dips and valleys I want to explore until dawn, but instead I'm frozen in place while my mind tries to process just how fucked I truly am.

Be it circumstances, coincidence, or plain old mutual horniness, sex on or before a first date has been pretty standard for me. Sometimes it would lead to something. More often it wouldn't. But I've never had to wait for it, never had to chase, and never had the experience of falling for a woman before falling into bed.

This is new territory for me, and it's terrifying. The pressure to make this as good for her as I know it's going to be for me is high because I like Ryan. Like her enough to more than like her, whether I'm willing to admit it out loud or not. Not only that, I know the woman standing here watching me with dark, heated eyes. I know she's a perfectionist and she lies about having a mustard allergy when she orders burgers because she can't stand the taste. I know she taps out the same alternating rhythm on her thigh when she's impatient and has a weakness for cheap white chocolate. I've seen her devotion to her job and her mom, and I want to know what it's like to have that intensity directed toward me.

This isn't an impromptu fuck after a night of flirting and drunken dance-floor groping. I'm not looking for a release for the adrenaline pumping through my veins after a kickass competition win. This is Ryan trusting me, lowering another of her walls, and the magnitude of it isn't lost on me no matter how hot I am for her.

I need to be careful with her. Gentle. Slow. I have to show her she means more to me than a weekend fling or a one-night stand.

I release the tight grip I have on her hips and let my hands slide along her smooth thighs. Her skin is insanely soft and smooth, her scent a combination of my soap and her lavender lotion. Unable to resist any longer, I kiss my way up her body, stopping to pay homage to the best breasts I've ever had the pleasure to lick while my knuckles graze along the lace trim of her underwear. My lips meet hers again, and I slip my hand under the delicate fabric, running my fingers through her folds.

"You're so fucking wet for me." I moan into her throat as I circle her clit and her hips rock against my hand. "Tell me what you want."

Her eyes are closed, and she grasps the neckline of my shirt with both small fists while I tease her. But she doesn't answer.

I flick my tongue along the gentle slope of her neck and nibble her earlobe as I ease two fingers inside her tight heat. "Tell me."

The only reply I receive is a quiet whimper while she grinds against my palm, seeking the release I'm desperate to give her. I'm shaking with the effort to go slow and keep my touch soft when every instinct I have is screaming to take her rough and hard.

I've never been big on talking during sex, yet I can't seem to stop now. I want to know how to please her, how to make her scream my name. I can feel her tightening around my fingers as her breathing becomes quicker, shallower. She drops her forehead to my shoulder, and one of her hands grasps my bicep. Her body is giving me all the cues I need to send her over the edge, but I can't ignore the feeling she's holding back.

"Come on, baby." I groan, pressing my aching cock against her hip and nearly detonating when her nails scrape against my skin. "You're so fucking beautiful. Tell me what you need."

"Oh God, yes. Right there." She finally gasps when I curl my fingers and graze her G-spot. "Harder."

Six words and I'm a man on a mission, determined to give my woman exactly what she demands. Screw sweet and slow. I wrap my fist around her hair, tug her head back, and plunder her mouth while I work her fast and rough. I'm drowning in the sounds she's making as her leg lifts and her heel digs into my ass. Her moans and incoherent pleas spur me on until she goes completely silent, and I feel the flutters of her cresting orgasm.

"That's it." I pant against her lips as the first violent waves shudder through her and she cries out. "Give it all to me, baby."

Watching Ryan come undone and knowing I did this to her snaps the last of my control. As she starts to go limp, I scoop her up and spin, all but throwing her onto the bed as I haul my shirt over my head and shove my board shorts off.

I know I'll regret not pausing long enough to enjoy the ravenous desire in her eyes as she takes in the sight of me for the first time, but my mind is on one track, and that train isn't taking the scenic route right now. I hook my thumbs in the lace of her underwear, exhaling a trembling breath when she lifts her ass and I peel them off her body. Crawling up the bed with zero finesse, I devour her lips and tongue, groaning as she explores my chest, tickles down my ribs to my hips, and wraps her warm hand around my cock.

"Oh wow." She breathes out as her fingers skim the three barbells running down my shaft. "I'm going to enjoy these."

I lock my shaking arms on either side of her head and look down to watch her pump me. Her grip is soft, her movements smoother and more graceful than my solo jerk sessions in the shower. I tear my gaze away to admire the view of her parted thighs open and waiting for me.

The view is hot as hell.

If this was our third or fourth time together, I wouldn't object to coming with her delicate little hand wrapped around me. But the apex of her thighs is calling to me like a damn siren song. Reaching over to grab the condoms out of my bedside drawer, I shift, her grasp on me tightens, and my knees almost give out.

"Fuck." I gasp, covering her hand with mine to still her movements. "I'm way too close."

She bites her lip, and I catch a satisfied glint in her gaze.

The unopened box of condoms does its best to cock-block me, but it's no match for Ryan. Laughing, she takes it, pops the side, and tears one of the foil packets off the strip. Without hesitation, she rips it open and, taking care to avoid tearing the condom on the barbells, sheaths me like a pro.

I can't think on that. Not when I'm already a grunting, territorial beast. Instead, I line myself up with her entrance and still until her eyes meet mine.

And I'm done. Officially fucked without officially fucking because no woman has ever looked at me the way Ryan is right now. A raging desire darkens her chocolate eyes, but beneath it is a gut-punch mix of trust, a hint of fear, and something way too close to mirroring how I feel about this woman.

"Are you sure about this?" I ask, brushing her hair off her forehead. "We can stop. Go watch another movie."

The fear evaporates, and she lifts her head to kiss me softly. "I want you, Malcolm. I just—" Her pause seizes my heart before she continues. "I want it to be good for you."

I drop my forehead to hers, chuckling. "Considering I'm so hot for you I'm probably going to last thirty seconds, I think that should be my line."

She smiles, and I start pushing inside her, squeezing my eyes shut as I sink into her tight, wet heat. When I'm fully inside her, I take a moment to try and regain what little restraint I can until I feel her grab my ass and dig her nails in.

"Fuck me, Malcolm," she whispers as she arches her back and places her hands above her head, submitting control to me. "Show me what those piercings can do."

With a ragged exhale, I give her what she wants. I'm not sweet or soft about the way I pound into her, pushing her farther and farther up the mattress until she's bracing herself against my headboard. I'm cursing and panting, my body slick with sweat as I fight off my own orgasm in favor of drawing another out of her. I lift her hips and flatten my palm on the wall for leverage.

The change in angle places the barbells into the perfect spot and brings about her telltale silence moments before she falls over the edge with a hoarse cry. "God, Malcolm. Please, yes!"

I detonate like a goddamn firecracker. My hearing, my vision, my mind—all of it goes offline as the most intense orgasm of my life takes over. I'm barely alert enough to brace most of my weight on my arms as I collapse onto her and roll to the side, my chest heaving.

"Damn," I mutter, rubbing my hands over my face to try and get the feeling back. "We are definitely doing that again."

Chapter Fifteen

Ryan

I'm staring absently at my computer screen when Renna finds me Monday morning. Fourteen tabs are open, and not a single one is able to hold my attention long enough to keep me from daydreaming about Malcolm.

The weekend-long marathon sex session isn't the only thing occupying my mind. It's the way he woke me Sunday morning to join him at the beach, a wetsuit in my size in one hand and a cup of coffee in the other. It's the low rumble of his laughter every time we moved from his bed to the couch to try and watch another movie. It's the look in his eyes when we went tandem on his board, and I moved from a panicked crouch to a shaky stance.

"So who is he?"

Blinking, I snap into reality and realize my secretary is sitting on my desk, watching me expectantly. "He?"

"Whoever you met while you were MIA last week. The guy making you zone out and smile at the dying ficus tree in the corner."

I glance at the time and subtly flip my phone over to hide the screen in case Malcolm texts me after his morning training. "There's no he. So where are we in rescheduling all the training sessions I missed? We should consider running a few group lessons since none of these guys have any serious deficiencies."

"Did it Friday." Renna taps at her phone, and mine dings. "Your new schedule for the week should be updated. Now who is he? Some middle-America cattle farmer? A rebel cowboy? I could totally see you going a little starry over some buff rancher."

Standing, I gesture to my attire. "What part of this outfit screams pickup truck and the smell of bovine in the morning?"

Renna assesses my emerald silk blouse and black pencil skirt, going so far as to hop off the desk and circle me. "Opposites attract."

"Sure they do," I scoff, hoping she can't see through my pathetic acting. "I better head down to the dance studio. We have two new recruits meeting me in ten minutes."

She lets me pass without further inquisition, and I breathe a sigh of relief when the elevator doors close.

I need to come clean to her. To Malcolm. I'm straddling two lives, and the deception hurts me as much as the truth will hurt them when I finally work up the nerve to admit to every little white lie I've told.

My guilt was kept at bay all weekend, rearing up only during quiet moments in bed when his arms would tighten around me before he fell asleep. I was alone in my penthouse last night at the top of this building when it finally took root again, wrapping its tendrils around my ankles and keeping me awake and pinned under my blanket long into the early morning hours.

But I can't simply call him up and tell him. Or show up on the beach and lay it out. An admission of this magnitude will need hours for discussion and explanation, not something to be done on the fly when there are distractions or pending appointments. Timing will be everything if I have any hope of salvaging things—like my heart—with Malcolm.

I study my calendar while I walk into the makeshift dance studio, searching for an evening Malcolm and I are both free and coming up empty for any date in the next four weeks. His afternoons and evenings are booked solid, much like my own. I make a few clandestine notes on my schedule of the nights he'll be home before midnight and close it out before sending him a quick hello and getting to work.

****

Malcolm

Jeremiah waits in the queue beside me while we study the techniques of the other dawnies riding the waves before the sunseekers arrive on the beach for the day.

"You're looking good in the curl," he says nonchalantly, like he hasn't been making subtle comments about my improved skill all week. "If I didn't know better, I'd be sizing you up for the August trials."

"Might not be a bad idea to know your competition," I reply, cringing when two surfers pop into the same wave and narrowly miss a collision.

His foot makes contact with my board, causing it to rock. "No way."

Glancing over at him, I grin. "Way. But word's not out yet, so keep it on the down, okay?"

The expression on his face eases any apprehension I had over telling my best friend, former competitor, and future challenger I'm aiming for a comeback. "Holy shit, man! It'll be so fucking awesome riding the circuit together again." He's downright giddy, bouncing on his knees. "And without a wife keeping your balls in a vice, you and me are going to do those after-parties up right this time."

I snort and shake my head. "I'm not doing this for the pussy."

His confusion is palpable. "Why not? I mean, yeah, win, but after taking the top slot, you have a duty to the sport and womankind everywhere, Cole."

I have to laugh at his seriousness. "Whatever. All I want is the chance to compete again."

"And getting laid is just the bonus level." He nods sagely until he suddenly stops, squints, and shakes his head. "Aw hell, no. No, Cole. No."

"No what?"

"This." He moans, gesturing at me. "How did I miss it? The smiling. The energy. The broken hottie radar. We've had a white bikini with a C-cup watching us all morning, and you didn't even notice, did you?"

Eyeing the incoming waves, I flip onto my stomach. "I'm focused."

"You're in love." He paddles into my peripheral and shudders. "And I think it's actually real this time, isn't it? Who is it? The chick you had over last month? The one you changed your sheets for?"

Frowning, I lose track of the wave I was watching. "What do you mean, actually real?"

His face twists up like it does every time my ex-wife enters the conversation. "Come on. You can't tell me that disaster of a marriage you had was based on anything other than sex and maybe too much booze. You didn't love Cara. I've been there, Cole. And where you two were wasn't it. Now, who is she?"

I charge ahead and take the next wave, getting in a

decent aerial before riding it in. Jeremiah is hot on my heels as I cross the surf to the sand and shake the water from my hair, noticing the blonde in the white bikini when cold water hits her, and she squeals.

"Sorry," I call over as I pass, snickering when Jeremiah stops to issue a more sincere apology and drop his name.

He keeps his opinions to himself while we swing by Barreled to check on Emma and Wade, but can't hold his tongue once we're on my rooftop with two breakfast sandwiches in hand.

"So?"

"So, what?" I huff, a little on edge with the knowledge it's been five days since I've seen Ryan and the time apart is not sitting well with me. "I met a woman. We clicked. Now we're seeing where it leads."

It's a total lie, and he sees through it.

Ryan and I didn't click. We fucking ignited. My phone is permanently attached to my hand now, and I'm like Pavlov's dog with the way I salivate every time she texts or calls. We both work tonight, but we should be done around ten, and the countdown has begun.

Jeremiah grunts and looks over the edge of the deck. "Just promise me you won't let this chick work you over like Cara did, okay?"

The thought of Ryan doing anything remotely duplicitous has me chuckling. I've seen her lie to a street vendor about the quality of his hot dogs, and it was the opposite of convincing. She doesn't have a deceitful bone in her body. "Trust me, she is nothing like Cara."

He's right about one thing, though. This thing between me and Ryan is different. Special. With Cara, I never looked past the next week or month, but when I think ahead to the future now, I see Ryan and a two-story house and a couple of dark-haired kids with big brown eyes and little clipboards in their hands.

I snicker to myself as he drops the subject, moving on to the more important news of my anticipated comeback and how my skills are stacking up against the guys we'll be going head-to-head with. By the time he takes off to let me get ready for my date, my confidence is solid.

Kaliah is still one of my favorite clients. She meets me at a movie premiere and spends the next six hours feeding me and introducing me to dozens of B-list celebrities. While she hasn't outright asked, I notice that she steers me toward the men and away from every woman under forty.

I appreciate her even more for it.

Once she's safe inside her limo, I wave her off and grab my phone, grinning like a moron when I see two messages from Ryan sent five minutes ago.

She's done working.

She's on her way over.

I text her a quick acknowledgment, hop in the truck, and make killer time on the freeways. I arrive home with barely enough time to run down the block and meet her at the corner.

"You look incredible," I murmur against her lips as I drag her close and sling her overnight bag onto my shoulder. "Ready to watch the sunset?"

"I thought you'd never ask."

Five days without her was going to be tough no matter what, but getting through the last three was damn near impossible. One late-night whispered curiosity about board sex, and I couldn't hit the water without some serious focus on keeping my hyperactive dick down. Energy I should have been spending reading the curvatures of the waves was funneled into not getting arrested for public indecency, and I admit my training suffered a little.

In no time, she's dressed in nothing but a little black bikini. The heat of the summer day still warms the sand and air despite the slow setting of the sun, but I grab a blanket anyway in case she gets cold on the way back.

"Are you sure it's safe?" she asks as we step into the surf and the cool water laps at our ankles. "We won't drown, right?"

Adjusting the board under my arm, I take her hand in mine. "I know every inch of this stretch of beach, and we aren't going out far." I lean down and kiss the top of her head. "I promise to keep you safe from the sharks."

"I know you will."

Once the board fin clears the ground, she crawls on and I dive in, surfacing to her laughter as I push the board—and her—into deeper water to a spot where the evening beach goers won't venture so close to dark.

I hop onto the board behind her, pull her in tight, and feel her shiver from the cold water soaking my hair and shorts. "You sure you're going to be warm enough? We can go back for the blanket."

"No way." She sighs, leaning against my chest. "This is absolutely perfect."

She's right.

The sun starts to drop, sinking beneath the rolling waves on the horizon. The sky is a symphony of color, turning the few white clouds bright shades of pink and orange. It's been a long time since I've been out here at night, and the view takes my breath away, made infinitely better by the woman in my arms. Everything feels like it should, as if the rest of my life was building up to this single moment where all the pieces finally fit together.

A large wave rocks the board, but Ryan doesn't tense. Instead, she presses her ass tighter against my half-hard dick and arches her neck so I can kiss her under the sliver of moonlight illuminating her smooth skin. Her tongue dances leisurely with mine, and I ease one hand into the cup of her bikini top to tease her taut nipple with my thumb while my other hand slips under the thin fabric of her bottoms. She squirms, and her thighs part for me, her kisses becoming more demanding as I slide my fingers through her wetness.

"What if someone sees us?" She pants as I circle her clit and nip at her neck.

Rocking my hips against her ass to relieve some of the pressure building in my spine, I adjust my slightly awkward angle and push two fingers inside her tight heat. "Too dark," I growl, doing a cursory scan of our location in relation to the pier. "Do you think I'd let anyone see you like this? Wet and spread open for me while I finger fuck you?"

She inhales sharply, grasps my wrist, and starts riding my hand.

I know it turns her on when I talk to her. She likes it when I tell her what I'm going to do and how much I love doing it. Whether it's the reassurance she needs to let go or something to keep her out of her head, it works every time.

And I fucking love it.

I tug on her plump bottom lip with my teeth and grind against her. "Can you feel what you're doing to me? How hard you make me?"

She whimpers something that sounds like yes, and I pinch her nipple, rolling it between my thumb and forefinger. Her core starts to tighten around my fingers, and her nails dig into my wrist as I still.

"Not yet," I murmur into her ear when she huffs with impatience and need. "Trust me."

The board beneath us rocks when I nudge her forward and plant my heels on either side of her hips. I lie back and hold my hands out to steady her as she turns on her knees. "Straddle me."

That sexy lip bite returns as she glances toward shore but doesn't hesitate. Her fingers splay across my chest for balance while I reach into the pocket of my board shorts and pull out a condom.

"I'm on the pill," she says quietly, tucking her hair behind her ear nervously like she's afraid I'll balk at the idea of going bare with her.

My cock pulses with the thought of feeling her without a single barrier between us. "I'm tested and clean."

Her eyes meet mine.

We're crossing a line here, one I've never crossed even while married and one I doubt she's crossed either. She's trusting me with her body as much as I'm trusting her with mine. And we're taking a real risk. One missed pill, one chance of being in that tiny percentage of failure and we'll be linked forever.

The thought doesn't petrify me quite like it should.

Her small hand slides under the band of my shorts and wraps around my cock, pumping it a few times while I hook my thumb in her bikini bottoms and move them aside. She lines us up and sinks down slowly, her eyes closing and lips parting as I fill her completely.

The change in temperature from cold and damp to hot and wet nearly has me coming before I'm fully sheathed inside her. Using my shoulder for leverage, she starts to move. She rides me slow at first, every rise and fall of her hips sending electric charges through my body while I grunt out one-word encouragements. Her head drops into the crook of my neck as her tempo increases until she goes silent and still.

Grabbing her hips, I take over, thrusting up into her at a punishing pace. "You gotta come for me, baby." I groan.

Between the rocking of the waves, the eroticism of making love to her out here on the ocean, and the sensation of being bare inside her, I can't hold back my orgasm. It rips through me, sending my hips slamming up into her as her own release follows mine. She's quiet, channeling her ecstasy through her nails as they rake down my biceps. The combination of pleasure and pain sends intense aftershocks through me until she collapses on top of me with a contented sigh.

"Good?" I ask with a grin as she traces light trails along my throat to my jaw.

"Very." She clings to me for a moment before easing off me and straightening her bikini. "I hope you saved enough energy to push us back."

Chapter Sixteen

Ryan

Renna looks over my shoulder as I rearrange my schedule, her thin brows furrowed. "Are you sure you have the time for this?"

"No," I reply honestly, cutting the last of this evening's appointments and shuffling them to Thursday. "But it's a solid opportunity, and I'd be a fool to miss out on it."

She picks up the papers scattered across my desk and arranges them into a single pile. "It's risky, taking on a building with an existing business. What do you intend to do with it? Beachfront commercial properties can't be flipped into residential without jumping through years of red tape, and the floor plan doesn't allow for office space rental like the rest of your acquisitions."

Checking my phone for confirmation my schedule changes will work for the employees affected, I take the stack from her hands. "I'll sit on it. Maybe hire a manager to oversee whatever business can turn a profit in that location until I'm ready to sell." Giving her my most confident smile, I shrug. "You said so yourself— it's beachfront. Beachfront property is never a bad investment."

"If it adds to your insane work hours, it is." She scrolls through her phone, and mine chimes moments later. "These are the most recent client reviews on social media. All positive. The influencers we comped dates for free are making good on their promises to sell Doll Parts to their followers, and according to Brit, our website is seeing triple our usual traffic."

Nodding, I scan for keywords. "Forward me our top ten resumes, and I'll narrow it down. We'll need to boost our product line if our current one can't keep up with demand."

"Will do." She pauses for a moment. "If you're serious about buying that business, maybe you should consider hiring a manager or two for here."

I lift a brow. "No."

She follows me out of my office where I'm saved from further interrogation by a gorgeous specimen of a man stepping out of the elevator. His dark eyes are as devilish as the smirk on his face, and I glance over my shoulder at Renna, biting the inside of my cheek when I see she's already shifted into Ballbusting Interviewer mode.

"Good luck," I whisper to the guy whose confidence has taken a slight dip under the scrutiny of Renna's unimpressed glare. "I hear she's the one you have to beat before you reach the boss fight."

His cocky smile is more forced as I pass him, and the elevator doors slide shut.

Firing off a text to Malcolm confirming I'll be by around ten tonight, I strut through the lobby and into the waiting car. I fold my legs inside, and my driver closes the door behind me. With a quick reminder of my change of plans, I put the divider up and take my compact from my purse.

All my research says Billy Sullivan is not a man who

will be impressed by an intelligent, well-dressed woman, no matter how healthy her bank account is. For tonight's meeting, I need to toss professionalism aside, play on his weaknesses, and strike from his blind side. I unbutton the top three buttons of my cherry-red blouse and tug my black camisole up an inch to provide the illusion of modesty. I shimmy out of my stockings, switch out my black pumps for red stilettos, and hike my skirt up an extra inch. A quick swipe of blood-red lipstick, a shaking upside-down hair flip, and a dusting of charcoal eyeshadow and I'm ready moments before we pull up to the trendy lounge Billy suggested for our meeting.

"I'll be no longer than two hours," I tell my driver as I exit the car and tuck my phone into my purse. "Make sure you eat during the downtime and charge it to Doll Parts's account."

I make it three steps before I catch sight of my reflection in the lounge's glass exterior, and my nerves begin to flutter in my stomach.

I'm breaking every rule of business I've held for myself tonight. Every piece of the powerhouse I've built myself into is gone as I walk inside and scan through the ambient lighting for a man whose face I'd know anywhere thanks to the hours of video and interviews I've watched over the last three days.

"Adrian Dawson?"

I feel his hand on the small of my back moments before I hear his voice, and I plaster a flirtatious smile on my face as I turn. "Mr. Billy Sullivan," I greet him, holding out my hand and swallowing my disgust when he gives me a blatant appraisal as he shakes it. "Why don't we sit?"

He keeps a tight hold on my fingers and leads me to

a secluded booth in the corner. I sit first, subtly inching away when he slides in a little too close.

The physical resemblance between him and his son is striking, from the sun-streaked blond hair to the vibrant blue eyes and broad shoulders. From a distance it would be easy to mistake them, but I see—and sense—the differences immediately.

Where Malcolm's smile is bright with lighthearted humor, Billy's is sardonic and sly and screams of manipulation. The father's gaze is leering, lacking the heated admiration of the son's. And while Malcolm moves with the ease of a man comfortable in his skin, Billy is aware of every woman in the room as he orders himself a beer and takes it upon himself to request a glass of white wine for me.

"So you're a fan, hey?" he opens, stretching his arms out across the back of the booth.

Swirling my glass, I channel the coy woman who contacted him through social media yesterday afternoon. "The biggest. Your run at Bondi Beach is on my most-watched video list."

With the door swung open, Billy takes control of the discussion throughout appetizers and our meal. I memorized everything I could about him and his short career, so throwing in the odd comment and gushing praise is easy.

I can make out a faint slurring of his words by dessert when he reaches over and plays with a lock of my hair. "Your message said something about a business proposition. What kind of proposal do you have for me?"

The sexual innuendo drips off his tongue as he speaks to my cleavage, and I take the opportunity to move out of his grasp while I pull a folded paper from my purse. "Barreled," I state, smoothing the creased page. "I've had my eye on it for years. Ever since I learned it was where you bought your first board."

His expression shifts from lecherous to bored. "Oh. Yeah. I'm taking it over."

Not if I can help it.

Ensuring my eyes are as bright as my tone, I slide the paper over to him and bounce in place. "That's what I heard when I went by to make the owners an offer. And it got me thinking."

"Yeah?"

His lecherous gaze is back on my boobs, so the pressure to keep the disdain out of mine is off. "Yeah. I mean, your name will draw people, but you don't want to actually work there, do you? It just doesn't seem like your thing, you know."

Shrugging, he leans back and crosses his arms. "I have my reasons."

Your reasons are you're a loser and an asshole.

"So do I," I press. "I want to be a part of it. A part of the history you built on the beachfront. That place wouldn't be half as hot as it is now if it wasn't for you and your reputation. We both know it."

My flattery is getting me somewhere, but I'm not certain it's where I'm wanting to go when he signals for the bill.

"Maybe not, but I'm not looking to be bought out."

"Not bought out. I want to be your partner." When I'm met with the lift of his brow, I smile. "My granddaddy left me a huge inheritance, and this is it. This is what I want to spend it on. We can go in fifty-fifty. I'll take over the day-to-day operations, and you can be the marketing. The face of Barreled."

The words are sour on my tongue as I conjure up an image of Billy Sullivan's sneer lording over the waves Malcolm rides.

Billy licks his lips and nods. "What kind of experience do you have running a business?"

"What kind do you have?"

He stares me down as the server places the bill on the table, blinking only when I hand the waiter my little black credit card. "Touché. Okay, Adrian. Give me a few days to think about it, and I'll let you know."

Slinging my purse over my shoulder, I slip from the booth and drop a hundred dollar bill down to cover the tip. "We would make a good team, Billy. I know we would."

I give my hips an extra sway as I walk away, tracking his hungry gaze in the mirrored windows until he's out of my sight and I can breathe.

****

Malcolm

Wipeouts are a part of life for surfers.

Small, frantic hands assessing every square inch afterward are apparently a bonus I've missed out on until now.

"I'm fine." I laugh, shaking the water from my hair while Ryan cops what should be an unsexy feel of my ass but still manages to make my dick twitch. "Not a scratch."

"There are at least eleven scratches," she grumbles, kneeling down to check out my right calf, which took a bit of a drag along the ocean floor when I first went down. "And a lot of blood."

I glance down to see if it's worse than I thought but get distracted by the paleness of her face. "Whoa. Let's get you sitting." I motion for Jeremiah to bring me my bag, then spread out a towel, crouch down, and run my thumbs over her cheeks. "Does the sight of blood make you lightheaded?"

"The sight of blood after witnessing that fall apparently does," she says with a shaking breath. "Sorry."

I kiss her forehead and open a bottle of water for her. "I'm the one who should say sorry, making you panic like that. I should've warned you I would be trying a few new moves on competition-level waves this morning."

She takes a drink and cranes her neck to see the scrapes on my leg. When I actively keep them from her line of sight, she frowns. "Apology accepted."

I could get used to this, someone worrying about me and fussing over a few tiny cuts. Emma is the only other person in my life who ever fretted over minor things like pebbles embedded in my shins or board rash, but it was more motherly, followed by a lecture and the application of weird-smelling ointments she swore by.

I know Ryan needs to get to work soon, so I get to my feet and hold out my hand to help her up. "What are the chances you can come by tonight?"

Wrinkling her nose, she sighs. "Zero. Late night, early morning."

"I could come to you."

Her hesitation is brief, but it still kind of stings. "Didn't you say you're training every morning until the elimination rounds start?"

"Yeah, but—"

"No buts," she orders, placing a finger on my lips and grinning when I nip at it with a growl. "You have six weeks. Once you show everyone you're the top dog again, I promise to bring you home and lock you in my room for a whole weekend."

She has a point. Not a point I want to hear, but a valid one.

I can't afford to be distracted. Everything is in perfect balance right now. Would I like to spend more time with Ryan? Hell yes. But we'll have time for that once I nail a few wildcard spots on the competition circuit and solidify my place.

Walking her to the corner where her driver is waiting, I duck down and kiss her, rolling my eyes when I hear Jeremiah hooting and hollering way too close for comfort. "Sorry," I mutter against her lips. "I warned you he's a dumbass."

"He's sweet," she replies as she waves at him over my shoulder. "Call me after work tonight?"

"Always." I watch her car until it turns the corner, ignoring my idiot of a best friend's attempt to sneak up on me. "You're a moron."

"Nah," he scoffs as we head back toward the water. "I'm sweet. Your woman said so."

We're paddling out to get in line when I ask him the question on the tip of my tongue since I introduced the two on the beach at dawn today. "So? What do you think?"

Jeremiah and Ryan sat on the sand and chatted for a solid hour before he joined me on the waves. He claimed it was too cold, but I knew damn well he was itching to size her up.

He hops onto his board and makes me wait for his answer.

"Jer."

"All right, all right." He sighs dramatically. "I like

her. She didn't ask about you once the whole time we were talking."

"And that's good?"

He shrugs. "It means if she has questions about you, your past, or anything, she'll come to you, not someone else. I respect that."

Nodding, I try not to grin like the moron I accused him of being. "Me, too."

Chapter Seventeen

Ryan

I despise being strung along, especially when the stringer is a vindictive, incompetent asshole with a weakness for cheap beer and a penchant for reliving glory days I suspect he was too drunk to remember clearly.

My plan—and my life—is spiraling out of control. Between Billy's waffling, Malcolm, Doll Parts's exploding popularity, and the web of lies I've woven to keep everything from combusting, there are too many spinning plates to keep in the air.

Case in point, I'm sneaking out of my boyfriend's bed to text his dad at three a.m. confirming another dinner meeting while transferring data between the duplicate calendars I'm now keeping up, one Renna can access and one she can't.

Billy responds immediately, suggesting for the second time that I call him so he can better get to know his potential silent business partner.

The thought sends a cold shiver through my bones.

Going off what Billy has told me, Malcolm has no hope of outbidding his father. Billy has put everything on the line, liquidated his assets, and taken out loans to cover the rest. He has the cash in hand, and Malcolm will come up thirty to forty thousand short on a blind bid.

But I won't know for sure until I lay eyes on Billy's official financial documents, something he's playing coy about.

"Hey," a gruff, sleepy voice murmurs. "You okay?"

Powering off my phone, I turn to see Malcolm standing in his bedroom doorway, scratching at his bare chest. "Very. I just had to deal with an email that was keeping me awake." I walk over to him and snuggle in close as his arms wrap around me.

He nuzzles my hair. "You work too much."

"Pot, meet kettle."

He chuckles as he leads me back to his bed and spoons me. "If I make the pros and land a few endorsement deals, promise me you'll slow down."

My breath catches, and my blood warms. "Are you planning on keeping me around that long?"

He's silent for a moment before he rolls me onto my back and brushes his thumb along my bottom lip. "Truth?"

The word is a blade through my soul, but I nod.

His gaze moves to my lips and then back to my eyes. "Truth is I've fallen for you. Hard."

"How hard?" I ask with a little smile as I shift my hips beneath him.

He grins, showing off his dimple in the smattering of moonlight coming through his curtains. "Hard as in I love you."

I'm not prepared to hear those words. I have no point of reference for this, no memories to draw on. My mom has told me she loves me with her mouth while walking out the door. I have recollections of my grandfather saying it when I was a child. Renna hollers it into my ear when she's tipsy on craft beer. But hearing it from

Malcolm drills those three words into a spot in my heart I didn't know was empty.

And my response is as eloquent as only Malcolm can make me. "What?"

"I love you," he repeats with a smirk.

I'm having an internal freak-out, and I'm not a good enough actress to hide it from him.

His lips brush mine. "Breathe."

"I am. I do. I do, too. Love you, that is," I stammer before I groan and cover my face with my hands. "Why do I become such a dork around you?"

He grabs my hands and lifts them over my head, holding them there as he grinds against my center. "Because I'm hot and you love me."

My laugh becomes a moan as he captures both my wrists in one hand and slides the other under the thin silk of my underwear. "Truth."

****

Malcolm

Ragdolling in the ocean sucks. It's disorienting. My limbs flail, unable to find my way to the surface. And it's terrifying. Even when I come out unscathed, the memory of it stays with me long after I get my feet on solid ground.

Love feels an awful lot like the same thing.

Coming to terms with being in love with Ryan may have brought me some strange internal peace, but hearing those words echoed back to me by a woman who makes my pulse race and my head spin with a single smile? I'm a walking disaster.

A ridiculously happy walking disaster.

I can't concentrate for shit. I'm grinning like a fool everywhere I go. Life is great, even when it shouldn't be.

I'm looking at the future with Ryan Rose-colored lenses, and it's a damn good view for a guy who swore off the idea of building a life with anyone other than a cat and maybe a goldfish.

It's been a week. Seven days of living this new reality where Ryan Rose is not only my girlfriend, but the woman who loves me enough to text those words from my bed this morning while I was testing my skills against the choppy double waves, which did their best to kick my ass.

I check my phone and bring up the message for a quick surge of dopamine before I walk into Barreled to check on Emma.

"Malcolm, my boy," Wade calls out from the back room. "Come help me unbox these new boards."

I kiss Emma's cheek and grab one of her peanut butter crunch cookies on my way by to join Wade in the storeroom. "Nice. I might have you put a couple of these aside for me and Ryan."

"You and Ryan?" he asks, lifting his brows. "Buying a woman a board is a serious commitment."

"I know."

Wade narrows his eyes and stares me down before his face breaks into a wide smile. "Good. I like the way you've been walking since that woman came into your life." He passes me a box cutter. "You have three weeks, you know."

The reminder sits heavily on my shoulders. But not as heavily as it was a week ago. "Yeah. I'm working on it."

"How short of the entry bid are you?"

"Twenty grand."

The man's shoulders visibly flinch. "Malcolm."

I lift a stack of plastic-wrapped rash guards out of the box and set them on the shelf. "Trust me, I'm doing everything I can to get there."

I can't look Wade in the eye. He wants my dad to buy this place as much as I do, meaning both of us would rather lose our left nut than see Billy Sullivan's name on the sign. But we're both caught between a rock and a hard place. Wade can't afford to let it go for less. I can't afford to pay more.

And Billy's lurking around with enough to buy Wade out thanks to me and my past dumbass decisions.

Wade hands me a longboard. "Why don't you ask your lady friend to join in? If you're as serious about her as I think you are—"

"Nope." I set the board on a hanger, shake my head, and tuck my hair behind my ear. "You know damn well why I'm keeping her under the radar until the prelims are over and this place is mine."

Disappointment settles on Wade's face. "You give that man too much power. Always have. If you love this Ryan woman like you claim you do, you need to trust her."

With a bravado I'm not feeling, I shrug. "Trusting her isn't the issue."

We work in silence until I have to head upstairs to get ready for tonight's date, a last-minute change in my schedule requiring me to trade my board shorts for a suit and tie. Renna Merchant herself called, growling about her calendar app failing and guaranteeing she'll enter my hours by hand once the glitches are fixed.

Even if I wasn't up for a fancy evening over the carnival outing I was initially slotted to attend, my balls aren't big enough to deny Renna. She scares me, and I'm man enough to admit it.

I'm in my truck with my location plugged into the GPS when my phone rings, and I answer without checking the name. "Malcolm here."

"Hey, baby."

I wince at the sound of Cara's voice carrying through the speakers. "What do you want?"

"I was just thinking about you," she says.

I know she's twirling her hair around her finger from the flirtatious tone I recognize all too well.

"About us."

Signaling, I merge onto the freeway. "There's no us. Now what's up? Why are you calling me?"

A faint sniffling is followed by a shuddered breath, and I roll my eyes.

Yeah, I remember this, too. The drama, the tears, the practiced quiver of her lip, all of it a perfectly executed manipulation I could never imagine Ryan putting me through.

"Cut the crap, Cara." I sigh as traffic hits a standstill. "I'm busy."

The quiet sobs end immediately, and I hear the woman I met the day my marriage ended.

"He's divorcing me for another woman."

I try to summon something akin to empathy but come up lacking. "That sucks. But I really need to get going."

"Seriously?"

A text chimes in from Ryan, and I read it over while I'm waiting for the truck in front of me to creep forward. I fire off a quick heart and a thumbs-up emoji before dealing with the misery that is my ex-wife. "Look, Cara, you need to stop calling me. You made your choice, and frankly, I'm better off for it."

"But you and I—"

I groan, knowing what I need to do to put an end to this. "There's no you and I. There's no we. There's no us. And there never will be. Goodbye, Cara. Sorry about the divorce."

I hang up, tap on her info, and block her number.

Maybe it makes me an asshole, but I feel nothing. I can't find an ounce of remorse or nostalgia in my head or my heart. If anything, I'm annoyed my ex's name will be mentioned the next time I talk to Ryan, because I won't hide it from her, no matter how inconsequential Cara's call was. If I learned anything from my failed marriage, it's that secrets kill relationships, and hiding my ex's calls because it would be easier isn't worth risking what I've got with Ryan.

The traffic in my lane moves another few inches, but I see the cars to my left starting to chug along. Knowing it'll be at least thirty minutes, I call Ryan in the hopes of getting the "my ex called, and I blocked her" conversation over before she comes by tonight. The clipped business tone of her voicemail makes me smile. It's so formal and precise, a far cry from the hot mess she lets me in close enough to see.

"I can't wait to see you tonight," I say as the truck ahead of me starts moving at a half-decent pace. "Text me when you're on your way over. Love you."

Chapter Eighteen

Ryan

No woman moves as smoothly as one trying to untangle from the grabby hands of a man she cannot stand but has to tolerate.

"Have I told you how fucking sexy you are?" Billy murmurs in my ear while I lead him to our seats, his steps already unsteady from the four complimentary glasses of wine he consumed in the lobby. "We're going to be so hot together."

I toss him a tight smile and mentally curse myself for not demanding to see the financial documents the moment we met up outside. If it wasn't for my stupid attempt to be sly, I wouldn't be at this incredible wine reveal gala with an asshole for a date. Billy's wandering hands have made it impossible for me to enjoy the stunning decor transforming the banquet hall into a decadent blood-red and black boudoir theme. Silks and satins billow along the rafters and shimmer in the dim lights, the only white in the room the center display of the newest wines being celebrated tonight.

The dress I chose for tonight is stunning but wasted on the man at my side. Black lace over red satin, the off-the-shoulder style and waist-high side slit provide the perfect sexiness to the floor-length skirt and long sleeves. When I had it sent over last week, Malcolm's reaction was what I imagined, not that of his father.

Billy snakes his arm around my waist, and I fight against my gag reflex as we arrive at our table where two other couples are already seated. I swallow down my disgust and smile. "This is us."

Dressed in a suit and tie, Billy Sullivan is a good-looking man. He's tall, fit, and broad-shouldered, his blond hair slicked back and curling behind his ears. He has the swagger and the confidence of a man who adores the spotlight.

To the untrained eye, I can see why women smile easily at him, why they lean in closer when he speaks. He introduces us and pulls out my chair as he makes small talk with the men about the quality of the wine samplings, all the while doing every fuck-boy move in the book in clear view of the women.

At a glance, he's polished and suave. He smirks, runs his thumb along his bottom lip, gives a little wink here and there, and has no qualms about manspreading into the space of the woman to his right. His moves are calculated and practiced, each position struck for maximum effect and attention.

All I see is a wannabe Malcolm.

Tasting the white wine placed in front of me, I try to focus on the conversation but fail.

I don't want to be here. Not with him. But until our signatures are on the dotted lines of the agreements our lawyers are drafting, I have to play nice. I don't want him examining the clauses too closely, and the less reason I give him to question my motives in partnering with him, the quicker this will all be over.

His hand slips into the slit of my dress and rests on my thigh while he continues to schmooze. I swallow another gulp of wine, and although I can no longer summon the starstruck smile of a fan girl, I do manage to purse my lips into something he misreads as a come-on.

His thumb creeps higher up my thigh as he leans in. "What are the chances you're gonna let me consummate our deal?"

With a forced laugh, I ease his hand closer to my knee and go with the other personality he seems to like, the shy good girl. "I haven't even seen your paperwork, Billy," I chastise quietly, pretending to be scandalized and hating myself for playing this game. "Besides, you know this isn't that kind of partnership."

"Yet," he fires back with a wink before something catches his eyes behind me and he stills, a Cheshire cat grin spreading across his face moments later. "Adrian, honey?"

Bristling at the endearment, I finish the last of my wine and prepare for another of his pathetic attempts to flirt. "Yes?"

"I'd like you to meet my son, Cole. Cole, this is Adrian, my beautiful date, business partner, and biggest fan."

****

Malcolm

No one warned me about the weird shit that would happen to my mind when I fell in love. They didn't tell me I'd sense the other person in a space long before I saw them or that I'd recognize them in a crowd by the tiniest, most inconsequential details. There's no talk of hearing their voice over a hundred others or picking up their scent from across the room.

Intel like that would've been very fucking helpful

eighteen seconds ago.

Instead, I'm staring past the slope of a shoulder I'd know anywhere into the smug face of my asshole father while my date for the evening tucks herself in tight beside me. My gaze follows the path of my dad's arm down to his hand where his fingers are digging into the skin of a smooth thigh I would recognize while blindfolded in a dark room.

There's a strange disconnect happening in this moment, one where what I'm seeing isn't matching what my brain is accepting. The woman swallows, and my eyes follow the curve of her familiar throat before studying a profile I know better than my own.

But it's still not clicking.

She turns toward me and looks up. Her eyes are speaking to me, but I don't understand the language. Rising to her feet, the woman extends her hand to me, this stranger with Ryan's face and body and scent. "Pleased to meet you, Cole. I'm Adrian."

It's not registering. She's breathtaking in a red-and-black designer dress that perfectly showcases amazing curves I could draw in my sleep, but I can't seem to reconcile the visual with the pieces slowly starting to fit together.

My body moves on rote training alone, and I take her hand, lifting it to my lips to kiss it as I would with any woman who offered her hand. "Pleasure to meet you." My voice is low and hoarse from the tightness in my throat and chest. "Call me Malcolm."

Her breath hitches, and the sound strikes a final shattering blow to the stupor I'm in.

My Ryan is here. With my father.

With my father, whose hand is slipping around her

waist as he stands and presses himself tight to her ass.

My fingers flex and crack before curling into a fist.

"Adrian Dawson? *The* Adrian Dawson?" my date exclaims. "I'm Amy. Amy Mulvaney. We spoke a few days ago about doing monthly employee features on my lifestyle blog."

I'm frozen inside the red fog I'm inhaling with every breath.

Adrian Dawson.

The Adrian Dawson.

The CEO of Doll Parts. The signature on my paychecks.

I know of Adrian Dawson.

Her eyes lift to mine. I see every lie she told me laid bare in her stoic expression, and I realize I know nothing of Ryan Rose.

"Oh, yes. Of course," Ryan—Adrian—says as her gaze rips from mine, and she slips from Billy's hold. "I trust you're having a good evening?"

"The best," Amy gushes as she places a hand on my chest and looks up at me. "Wouldn't it be great if one of these couples would trade places with us so you can catch up with your dad and Adrian and I can talk?"

Billy's attention is on Amy's plunging neckline, and I want nothing more than to smack the smirk off his face as he speaks directly to her cleavage like he doesn't have Ryan at his side looking like the siren she is.

"Why don't you make it happen, sweetheart?"

Ryan turns, and my gaze moves along the smooth line of her hips. Hips I was gripping while I pounded into her seventeen hours ago.

I can't look away from the sight of her hair falling in wild curls down her back as her calm, collected voice slams into my skull. "Tonight is about us, Billy. We have things to discuss, and it's in both our best interests if Cole isn't around to hear it."

My father's grin is lecherous as he nods and shrugs. "You heard the lady, son. We'll catch up another time."

****

Ryan

Clap. Smile. Nod. Repeat.

Clap. Smile. Nod. Repeat.

My mantra carries me through the wine showcase and speeches, past the samplings, and into this moment where Billy's weight is threatening to crumple me as I guide him to his waiting taxi.

"May I?"

I blink to keep the tears from falling at the sound of Malcolm's voice rumbling low behind me. "I've got it."

His muscled arm slides under his father's, and he accepts the burden silently, escorting Billy into the backseat and closing the door. The cab pulls away from the curb, but he doesn't turn, doesn't walk away, doesn't move.

The music of the gala rides the warm breeze, a cheery beat serving as a soundtrack to my self-inflicted heartbreak. "Malcolm."

"Don't," he finally says quietly as he slides his hands into his pockets and tilts his head toward the dark sky.

My chest aches with a pain I've never felt. It's loss. Longing. Rage and regret and fear. Every lie I told is on the tip of my tongue, desperate for a forgiveness I don't deserve. "I—"

His shoulders slump, and he shoves his hands through his hair. "I don't want to hear it, Ryan—Adrian.

172

Whatever you think you need to say, don't. Whatever you think you need to do, don't. Just—" His voice cracks, and he clears his throat. "Just don't, okay?"

And then he walks away.

My heart is pounding like it's trying to leap from my body and return to him where it belongs. Words of apology and remorse form and die on my tongue before I can speak them. I'm rendered immobile as everything collapses around me, rooted to the spot by an anchor of my own making and forced to watch him until he disappears around the corner.

My hands shake as I take my phone from my clutch and call my driver to pick me up.

I can do this.

I can hold it together for thirty more minutes.

I can keep my head high and my shoulders back and my tears unshed until I'm home. There are too many people here, too many witnesses to the breakdown I feel building like a tsunami in my mind.

Twenty-four minutes.

My driver doesn't speak when he arrives. He follows my lead and allows the silence to hang thick in the air until he reaches the freeway.

"Home or the boardwalk, ma'am?"

"Home, please."

Fourteen minutes.

My feet carry me through the Doll Parts lobby and into the elevator. Muscle memory pushes the code to my penthouse. I set my keys and clutch on the redwood table in my entranceway, lock my door, and walk through my home on autopilot.

I have no laundry, dishes, or cleaning to do thanks to my housekeeper, Evelyn. There are no pets to feed or plants to water, no television to distract me. I ensure my emergency dress and heels are prepped in my office, the outfit selected to exude power should one of the evening bookings take a turn and require my presence. So far, I've made use of it exactly once thanks to a distraught client who called me instead of an ambulance when her date had an allergic reaction to her homemade white clam sauce, but the preparation gives me the sense of control I like.

Or, more accurately, need.

Except I have none as I sink to my knees in the silence of my penthouse and cry.

Chapter Nineteen

Malcolm

Appearance: three stars.

I close out the Doll Parts app, set my phone on the bathroom counter, run my hand over my unshaven jaw, and tilt my chin up to get a better look at my bloodshot eyes before admitting three stars was rather generous of the woman I escorted to a wedding yesterday.

"I'm calling in an order for Indian fusion," Jeremiah calls from my living room where his ass has been planted since The Gala Incident. "Want any?"

Lathering up, I start the process of removing the two weeks' worth of scruff. "I have a date. Some library auction thing."

He snorts, and I don't disagree with him.

Continuing to work for Adrian Dawson has been a real mindfuck, and I can't say I'm sorry tonight is my last date. I called Doll Parts two days after The Incident, determined to quit on the spot. Ms. Merchant merely chuckled drily, told me there wasn't a chance in hell she'd release me without two weeks' notice, and sent me an updated schedule.

I shrug a gray blazer over my white shirt and check over my somewhat acceptable appearance one last time before I pass Jeremiah and grab my keys, wallet, and phone. "You know the rules."

"I know 'em, but I'm still not gonna follow 'em."

I flip him off, jog down the stairs, and slip into the alley behind Barreled where my truck is parked.

I haven't spoken to Wade or Emma since last week when I told them I was withdrawing from the bidding. Playing it off as a sound decision to focus my efforts on returning to the pro circuit, I talked up my recovery and training and yammered on about a few apartments I was scouting farther up the coast.

Then Wade asked about Ryan. I went full-on sullen mute. Emma cried.

Following my GPS, I weave through traffic and make it to the library in record time. The dark circles under my eyes might be a strike against me, but I'm definitely a solid four out of five tonight.

Smoothing my shirt down, I walk along the garden path leading to the entrance where a gorgeous brunette is holding two wineglasses and chatting with security at the door.

She catches my eye and smiles. "I'm Minda. You must be Malcolm." She licks her lips as she checks me out like one might a show dog. "You're even hotter than your profile pictures, which says a lot because you, honey, are very photogenic."

"Glad to know I don't disappoint in person," I say with a practiced grin as I take the wine she offers. "You look stunning this evening."

It's a rote response but not a lie. My date is one of those Amazonian women, tall and busty with legs for miles. Her bio lists her job as influencer, and standing here now, I think I do recognize her from somewhere. Her hair is long and sexed up, her makeup done for those smoky, sultry bedroom eyes and cock-sucking lips.

She's wearing a skintight black dress I doubt she'll be able to sit in, and she's definitely braless. Maybe even commando.

And my dick doesn't give a rat's ass. The traitor is still attached to the one woman he's never going near again. He and I have had more than one conversation about it, but he's a stubborn fucker.

Not that it matters tonight anyway. Work is work, and my job right now is to make sure Minda has a good time, gives me a decent final review for my ego's sake, and then I'm free of everything related to Adrian Dawson and Doll Parts.

Minda places her hand on my forearm, and her white-tipped nails rake softly over my skin. "Why don't we head inside? I'd like to look over the auction items once more before the bidding starts."

"Lead the way."

The grand entrance is sleek and modern with subtle signage directing people to the auction room, the displays, the table where silent auction bids are being taken, and the bar. Servers decked out in black and silver mingle with trays of hors d'oeuvres and complimentary wine. The place reeks of wealth and prestige, and I know I won't miss this part of the job one bit.

Minda is good company, and I'm on my best behavior. Some vindictive piece of me wants to see five stars across the board after tonight, a final see-what-you-missed kind of thing to Adrian Dawson. It's petty, sure, but feeling petty is a fuck of a lot better than the persistent dark fog I've been living in for the past fourteen days.

"This would be fun," my date announces, trailing her finger along a plaque describing a three-night resort vacation to the Maldives. "I wonder what Doll Parts would charge for a seventy-two-hour booking."

"Probably a lot," I say offhand, distracted by a faint, familiar scent filtering through the room.

Minda laughs as she puts her name and a number down on a slip of paper. "I'm banking on it being worth every penny."

She takes my hand and leads me into another room where the live auction items are available for perusal prior to the event. I feel a strange restlessness buzzing through my skin, and I tug at the collar of my shirt as subtly as I can, grateful when a server slows beside me long enough for me to take a bottle of chilled water.

"That must be a new one," Minda states, leaning in close to my ear. "Your boss is one lucky woman, getting to test drive all you sexy thangs before she lets the rest of us have a chance."

Since I'm apparently a masochist who enjoys reliving the newest worst moment of my life, I lock my expression into total disinterest and follow Minda's gaze to see Ryan standing across the room on the arm of a dead man walking.

At least this time it isn't my dad.

Her deception and betrayal is as fresh tonight as it was when she clawed me open two weeks ago, but my cock doesn't care. He's too busy staring at her curves encased in an off-the-shoulder turquoise dress, which fades to gold along the skirt. The way her legs are framed by the asymmetrical hemline makes her look like a mermaid. A siren.

It's fitting.

"I swear she has the best stylist in LA," Minda huffs with a hint of annoyance. "I've never seen Adrian

Dawson look anything other than perfect."

"I have," I mutter before I catch myself. Clearing my throat, I stop one of the servers and grab another two glasses of wine. "Why don't we go find a seat?"

My body is thrumming with adrenaline and anger and something I don't want to think about while Minda selects a table with the best lighting. I have to give a Herculean effort not to look over my shoulder, not to seek Ryan out and demand answers I doubt I want to hear.

Because that woman in the mermaid dress isn't her. They may share the same face and body, but the resemblance stops there. Adrian Dawson radiates an air of aloof unapproachability and cool detachment as she scans the room with bored, lifeless eyes. Her smile is as perfectly practiced as her pose, like she knows she's being watched and assessed and judged.

Which I suppose she is.

If I was a better man, I might summon some empathy for her, but I'm still living in the Land of Pettiness, so I tamp any hint of concern for her down and give it a metaphoric boot stomp for good measure.

Minda leans into me, angles her phone, and I smile on command. Her thumbs fly across her screen before she gives me a satisfied smile and shows me the photo. "Damn, we look good."

I hum in agreement because yeah, we do. Individually. Minda's gorgeous, and I'm no slouch, so sure, the picture looks decent. But it only reinforces something I realized last week during a moment of weakness.

I have no picture of us.

Or her.

After Cara, I spent hours ridding my camera roll and social media of the hundreds of pictures of my ex. Her selfies and posed shots took up an embarrassing amount of storage on my phone, but when it came to Ryan, there wasn't a single one for me to delete, and that sucked in its own way.

"How fast do you think he'll go into the rotation?" Minda muses beside me.

I can't help but glance two tables over at the brown-haired guy pushing Adrian's chair in for her while she perches on it like a queen surveying her subjects.

"Not that I want to trade down or anything, but I have a friend who just loves those tall, dark, and dangerous ones."

Dangerous, my ass.

The guy looks like a future back-shaver.

The auction starts, and Minda is right in there, tossing bids out and sighing with annoyance when she loses. Needing to escape for a few minutes, I excuse myself and head into the deserted lobby to get away from the noise, the energy, and a certain CEO.

I'm tucked behind a pillar, scrolling through a generic email from an upcoming competition, when the doors to the auction room open and the siren slips into the empty lobby. She looks around for a moment before she leans against the wall, squeezes her eyes shut, and clutches her purse to her chest. I can't look away while she takes a few deep, shaking breaths and bows her head, allowing her perfect curls to bounce forward and shield her face.

My phone buzzes, and she straightens in a heartbeat, smoothing her dress over her hips as she scans the area, her disinterested expression faltering when she sees me.

"Malcolm," she says, squaring her shoulders and tilting her chin. "Are you having a good evening?"

"The best," I reply, slipping my hands into my pockets so my aching fingers get the message her skin is off-limits. "You?"

"The best." She gives me a tight smile and peruses the quiet room. "I was just coming out for some air."

"Same." I clear my throat. "So did you see anything interesting to bid on?"

"Not really. You?"

"Nope."

I hate this. I hate everything about this. I hate how stilted and impersonal we are when mere weeks ago we were lying naked in my bed, watching superhero movies, eating taquitos, and arguing over why invisibility would be a kickass power compared to flying. I hate knowing she's feeling as awkward as I am, and I can't do anything about it.

I hate that she did this to us.

And I hate how much it hurts to see her looking so polished and unaffected and fake.

I know breakups are supposed to be painful, and maybe I'm a sucker for not being able to mesh Adrian Dawson with Ryan Rose, but this is a whole new level. I feel like the woman I fell in love with isn't even in the room, and it's throwing me. I can't think straight, not when I want to strip her out of her designer dress, mess up her hair, and toss one of my T-shirts on her so I can confront the woman who betrayed me.

But she isn't here, and Adrian Dawson is, and I need to know.

I push away from the pillar and stalk toward her. "Why?"

She licks her lips and tightens her hold on her purse. "Why what?"

"Why him?" I cage her with my arms, ready to back away if I sense a lick of fear in her but needing to see the truth in her eyes. "Why Billy, Ryan? You could have any man in LA. I—" I look to the ornate gold designs painted on the ceiling, like maybe they will give me the strength to survive her reply. "Why?"

"I have my reasons."

"Have," I echo as I back away, chuckling. I don't know why seeing her date tonight had me thinking my father was no longer in the picture, but it did, like I had some ridiculous hope lodged somewhere in my head that maybe, maybe, Billy was a one-off. A mistake. Maybe even forgivable.

But her reasons are still in play, and that means he is, too.

I run my hand through my hair then take a moment to straighten the sleeves of my jacket. "I hope they're worth it."

As I walk back inside the auction room, I hear her response.

"I hope so, too."

Chapter Twenty

Ryan

I look in the mirror, and I see my mother.

Not literally, because my coloring and face shape are nothing like hers, and she trends toward lean while my hips have been prepped for childbirth since puberty hit, but I am my mother's daughter in every way that matters.

Renna stands in my office, waiting for me to continue with interviews I never approved for jobs I didn't advertise.

"Bindy Allen is up next," she calls out as though she hasn't usurped my position as decision-maker for Doll Parts. "She has extensive experience in Silicon Valley and has a reputation for being a shark while negotiating benefit packages."

I touch up my lipstick and tilt my head to assess the faint lines around my eyes.

Billy Sullivan's crumpled financial documents are sitting on my desk beside a stack of resumes, and both are waiting for me to make my move.

Except I can't.

For the first time in my business career, I'm torn between two paths, and I don't know which to take. One keeps me safe and secure in this tower I've built from the ground up. It's familiar, a tiny piece of the world where the power rests in my palm. My entire life has centered around it for so long I can't imagine what my life would look like without it.

The other is a risk. A risk with a reward I may never reap.

"Ryan?"

I take one last glance at myself and exit the bathroom. "Why are you doing this?"

Renna doesn't flinch. Instead, she slips her phone into her pocket and stares me down. "Because I know about Malcolm."

Years of maintaining a stoic expression in the face of surprise serves me well. I cross the room and take my position at my desk. "Malcolm Sullivan? What about him?"

"You know he quit."

I nod and pretend to read over the qualifications of my next interviewee.

Of course I know. My chest is still empty from seeing him on his last night of work, from trying to mask my heartache and shame when he caged me between his arms and demanded to know why. Why Billy. Why his father. Why I ruined us. Even now, my lies cling to the tip of my tongue, desperate to be freed from the stubborn grasp I can't relinquish. Not yet.

"You know why he quit."

Giving her my best exasperated glare, I lean back. "Why?"

Renna throws the same look back at me. "You're actually going to sit there and keep lying to me," she states. "Me. The only person on this planet who was honest enough to tell you to your face honey blonde wasn't your shade. You're just going to pretend, like I

184

don't have your cycle programmed into my calendar and you don't have mine. Are you serious right now?"

I open my mouth to defend myself. "I love him."

If Renna is half as surprised by my confession as I am, she doesn't show it. She simply crouches in front of me. "And?"

"And what? We broke up. It's over. I love him, and it's over, and that's okay. I'm okay. Everything is fine. All of it. Everything."

Tears are falling down my cheeks, and I can't stop them any more than I can stop the truths from spilling out of me.

Between gulping sobs, I tell her everything. I tell her about our first date and surfing and meeting Carlos and Jeremiah. I confess to messaging him my phone number and tampering with the servers so Brit wouldn't find out. I unleash every worry I had about being discovered and each little white lie that snowballed into more. I cry over breaking down and scouring old surfing blogs for pictures of his ex-wife last week so I could see what he saw in her, and then I admit to flagging a photo on Minda Arrow's social media page for being inappropriate while sitting ten feet away from her at the auction because she was smiling and he was smiling and I was dying.

And then I tell her about Billy.

I tell her how my plan formed and who he is, how I was determined to know what his blind bid would be so Malcolm wouldn't lose, and how I planned to use the information to either convince Malcolm to let me help him or put in my own bid to trump them all. I tell her about the meetups with Billy and the breakup with Malcolm, and then I confess everything about my mom and my fear of becoming just like her because I damn near went out tire-slashing when I watched him leave with Minda and overheard the offer she giggled into his neck.

By the time I finish, I'm sitting on the floor with a run in my stockings and surrounded by a mountain of tissues. I'm exhausted and defeated and empty, except for one last admission.

"I don't want to be me anymore."

I don't have to elaborate. Renna has been here from the start. She remembers when I had time to go to the library and when I walked anywhere within a three-mile radius to save money. She was at my side while I scoured through secondhand shops for power suits and shoes that sent a message.

She was the one who bleached and then tinted my hair the night I decided I would be more successful as a honey blonde. And she was the one who fixed it with a six-dollar box dye in my one-room bachelorette pad with the accordion-style bathroom door.

Trying to salvage what's left of my shredded dignity, I begin to gather the tissues and put them in the trash. "Do you want to know the worst part?"

Renna remains on the floor, her attention on her phone. "Of course."

"With all the overtime lately, he would've won the bid. He never needed my help."

That gets a flash of mild intrigue. "Would've?"

Nodding, I slump back against my desk. "When Billy handed me his financials, he was positively crowing because he'd just received word Malcolm backed out." Chuckling without a stitch of humor, I stare at the ceiling. "One look at those documents and even a child could see Billy was all talk and no walk. He's made the minimum bid with ten dollars to spare. Ten. Dollars. I destroyed the best thing that ever happened to me for ten dollars."

Five years of paperwork told a bigger story, but I hadn't had the energy or the will to figure it out, because all that mattered was Malcolm walked away from his dream for nothing.

"Wow. Love really does make you stupid."

I glare at her. "It's genetic."

Renna full-out snort-laughs at me, at her best friend who just laid herself bare. "It's not genetic. Everyone is an idiot when they fall in love. Especially when it's their first time." She pats me on the knee and gives me an exaggerated pout before returning her attention to her phone. "Is your pity party done now?"

"Maybe it is. Or maybe this is how my life will go from now on." A horrible thought dawns on me. "What if this is how it started with my mom? What if one broken heart turned her from a perfectly reasonable, successful woman into this? Oh God. This is it, isn't it? One day, I'm going head-to-head against moguls for a downtown development, and the next I'm crying on the floor of my office, mourning the loss of little blond babies that don't even exist."

Renna groans long and loud, lolling her head back. "That's enough. Get up. You're a hot mess, emphasis on the mess."

"I'm sad," I growl, keeping my ass on the floor out of stubbornness.

"No, you're Adrian Dawson," she counters. "You don't sit on floors in wrinkled clothes surrounded by dirty tissues. You're Adrian Dawson, and you get shit done. You plan. You fix. You win. This—" She sighs, flapping her hand at me. "—is not you."

Grumbling, I push myself to my feet and slip my heels back on. "That's the problem, isn't it? I wasn't Adrian Dawson with Malcolm. I was Ryan Rose. When I was with him, things changed, and plans changed, and he helped me be okay with it. I wasn't five steps ahead of every game because I didn't have to be. I could just, I don't know, live."

Renna taps at her phone, and mine chimes. "It's called balance, Ryan. Balance and letting go. Check your updated calendar." She walks out.

I call to her before the door closes. "Renna?"

"Yes, boss?"

"I'm sorry."

"Prove it," she hollers over her shoulder. "Check your calendar."

Frowning as the door snicks shut, I pick up my phone and obey my best friend's order, sinking into my chair when I see the first item on the docket.

Step One: Forgive yourself, girl. You fucked up, just like the rest of us mere mortals. No one died. You'll live and so will we.

I take a deep, shuddering breath, knowing this step isn't going to happen. Not yet.

Step Two: Clean yourself up. You have mascara on your chin, lipstick in your eyebrows, and I did not source that skirt from Italy for you to roll around on the hardwood in it. Do better.

This one, I can accomplish.

I spend longer than expected to erase the evidence of my meltdown. My makeup requires a full redo once I get most of my post-cry swelling down. My hair needs a miracle to fix the tangles without frizzing it up. I have to accept the loss of my stockings, but I get it done.

Feeling a tiny bit better, I leave the bathroom to find a small charcuterie next to my laptop. With a pickle in hand, I prepare myself for my next task.

Step Three: Hire Bindy Allen and Yolanda Carlisle.

Firing off a text to Renna, I complete the job in under thirty seconds.

Step Four: Fuck Billy Sullivan over, then fuck Billy Sullivan up.

Attached to this is an address, a name, and a time.

Uncertainty takes hold, and I hesitate.

What if Malcolm didn't back out because of money but because he no longer wanted to be tied down to a business when his career is about to take off again?

What if I do this and he resents me for tainting Barreled with my deceptions?

Worse yet, what if I do this and he feels obligated to forgive me?

The half-eaten pickle is still in my hand when Renna opens my door and tosses her phone my way.

"Here," she says, tapping her screen as she snags a cracker and a slice of Swiss. "This should make your decision for you."

Ten minutes later, I'm out the door with my lawyer awaiting my call.

Chapter Twenty-One

Malcolm

Cinching the arms of my wetsuit around my hips, I shift my weight from foot to foot and watch the first heat paddle into line before I scan the growing crowd of observers filling Huntington Beach.

"Did you tell her about this?"

I pop the lid off my water bottle, take a drink, and ignore Jeremiah's question. "Who should we have our eye on in this round?"

"Gonzalez and Miller," he replies without hesitation. "If you aren't expecting her, why are you looking for her?"

Good fucking question.

It's been four long nights since I left the auction with Minda, determined to take her up on her offer of a no-strings romp. The idea was sound—a quick roll in the hay to relieve a little tension and get Ryan out of my head once and for all. Theoretically, Minda and I made sense. She wanted to fuck. I wanted to forget. Add a few glasses of wine and too many shots of tequila…

I return my gaze to the water as the buzzer sounds.

The problem with trying to fuck a woman out of my head is I have to be able to get it up for someone who isn't her. And that's where my plan fell apart.

I couldn't even kiss Minda. She moved in, I moved

away, she tried again, and I tossed up every ounce of booze I'd drunk that night into a garden a block away from the library.

The only good thing to come out of the disaster was Minda's discreet understanding of my drunken ramblings, ramblings I'm damn lucky she didn't add to her blog review of Doll Parts. The poor woman sat on a cement barrier for over an hour, listened to me yammer on about Ryan, and not once did she call me out for referring to Ryan as my soul mate in the same breath I cursed her name. Hell, she even rubbed my back while I lamented losing the woman I was going to marry someday in between hiccups, a few foul burps, and my barely coherent descriptions of kids I never had.

Shoving my hand through my hair, I realize I owe that woman flowers. Except I don't want to give some random woman flowers. Maybe a twenty-five-dollar gift card would suffice.

Jeremiah came to the rescue, driving into LA at three in the morning to pick up my sorry, drunk ass and carry it back to his apartment where I proceeded to dry heave for another thirty minutes.

His retribution came in a seven a.m. wakeup to hit the waves. He deserves zero flowers or gift cards.

"You gotta get your head in the game," he warns me, snapping me off the downward spiral I'm riding. "This is your shot. You can deal with the rest after."

He's right.

I hate him a little for it.

Bouncing on the balls of my feet, I hike my board under my arm and lie better than Adrian Fucking Dawson. "I'm ready."

He grins. "Let's fucking do this!"

I can't help but smile back as we hike out of the quiet cove and into the heart of the competition where surfers, fans, and onlookers are congregating. A hum ripples through the crowd the deeper we get as heads turn our way and phones lift.

Yeah, I'm back. And it should feel good.

The wildcard slot I secured lists me in the final heat alongside Jeremiah. It's a ploy on behalf of the organizers hoping to keep the attendees on-site until the end, the pitting of the reigning champion against a former one.

A photographer ducks into view, and Jeremiah swings his arm over my shoulder, stilling us long enough for a decent shot.

Getting caught up in the hype of a competition is easy. The music, the smells, the sounds of hardcore fans calling my name…all of it creates a surreal bubble where nothing else exists except for this and the waves.

And Ryan, who hovers in my head everywhere I go.

I don't know what it is about today, but that familiar buzz in my veins is present as Jeremiah and I enter the competitors' tent. It persists throughout our registration, making my wetsuit feel tight and constricting when I zip it up and fasten my number on it. Heat after heat wraps up, and I can't shake off the sensation.

"This is bullshit," I mutter under my breath when Jeremiah and I are called to the water for our warmup along with two other competitors.

Jeremiah shoulders me as he dives in. "Naw, man. This is it. Slay it out there."

This is it.

Following suit, I take one last look over my shoulder, hop onto my board, and accept the fact I've gone off the rails, because I swear to God I just spotted Ryan in the crowd.

****

Ryan

No.

No, no, no, no, no.

I may not know much about surfing, but I know staying upright and on the board is a big part of it, and that is the opposite of what Malcolm just did.

By the time he resurfaces, I'm pacing a small patch of sand unclaimed by a blanket, chair, towel, or umbrella and listening to the announcer's commentary.

"A disappointing warmup for Cole Sullivan on what is expected to be his comeback ride in today's wildcard position," the man calls through a loudspeaker, his voice distorted and tinny. "Sullivan has been absent from the competition circuit since his career-ending injury eighteen months ago when he took an unexpected cut out of the pocket and lost control."

"That was a tough watch, Garrett," a second man chimes in.

I want to knock both their heads together.

"Preliminary notes place Sullivan as a serious contender for world competition if he can recapture his style, but he's going to need to step up his game if he hopes to beat out Jeremiah Elkhorn."

"That he does, James. That he does."

I fire a death glare in the direction of the tower where Garrett and James are calling the event, but it does nothing to silence their musings as they move on to critiquing another surfer's aerial.

I clutch a thick stack of papers in my hands, squeezing them to center my nerves while Malcolm mounts his board and paddles out, shaking his head. He reaches the line and barely pauses before he hops up and grabs an incoming wave even I can tell is too weak for a decent showing.

"What is he doing?" I snarl, slapping the papers against my palm in frustration. "This isn't him."

"He's too deep into his own head," a grizzled voice posits to my right. "He'd be better off pulling out now and trying again in a few months."

I turn to defend Malcolm to the know-it-all beside me then freeze, wondering if his lawyer has contacted him yet. "Wade?"

"Hey. It's Ryan, right?"

I nod.

Barreled's owner crosses his arms, wincing when Malcolm miscalculates his angle and he wipes out. Again. "That boy is going to end up with an injury he can't come back from if he stays out there."

I can see Malcolm's frustration in the way he steadies his board with his hand and looks to the cloudless sky. "He's the best out there," I say weakly against the evidence. "Maybe it's just jitters."

Wade frowns and scans the crowd behind us. "If I didn't know better, I'd say those two are here screwing with his focus again."

The weight of my guilt is heavy on my shoulders. "Who?"

"Billy and Cara." He shakes his head as a whistle blows and Malcolm exits the water with the other competitors. "Stealing his money was one thing, but I never thought his own father would stoop so low as to steal his wife, too."

My eyes narrow as I stare straight ahead and bite my

tongue a little longer.

****

Malcolm

I'm losing it. Everything.

This competition.

My career.

Barreled.

Ryan.

My sanity must be next on the list, because I swear I hear her in the distance above the din of cheers, announcements, and general mayhem. Jeremiah is barking out what I'm sure he thinks is a pep talk, the organizers are trying to herd us in to review the rules before our heat begins, and two bikini-clad women are leaning far enough over the flimsy barrier to make me concerned they'll topple the tent.

And above it all, Ryan's voice stands out.

But so does my father's.

"Touch me again, and I will make it my personal mission to see you lose what's left of your pathetic savings," Ryan snarls, and my head snaps to the right.

"You fucked me over, bitch," Billy replies, his words slurred.

I slam my board against Jeremiah and vault over the barrier, ignoring the women shoving markers toward me while I scan the crowd and spot Ryan twenty yards off and moving away at a good pace. As the only woman on-site wearing high heels and a knee-length fitted white dress cinched with a thick black belt, she's impossible to miss.

"Did I ever," I hear her say while I push my way to her. "Some might call it karma. I call it the Adrian Dawson Special."

Billy is following her, barely keeping up as he stumbles through the sand. "What the fuck are you going on about?"

She turns to face him while I close in on them, and I slow to a stop when she licks her lips, looking him over with that cold, calculated gaze I saw at the auction.

"If I live for a thousand years, I will never understand how someone like you managed to father a man like Malcolm."

With a snort, Billy crosses his arms. "Man? Cole's nothing but a loser coasting on my name." He sneers as he tries and fails to match the pure revulsion on her face. "But as my biggest fan, I'd think you know that by now."

She takes a step toward him, and I move in sync, tracking Billy's every twitch in case he decides to lunge and I have to take a murder rap.

"I know a lot of things, Sullivan," she says with a Cheshire smile. "I know you lost your endorsements six months before Malcolm was born because no brand was willing to have their reputation damaged by association with an athlete who couldn't pass a piss test. I know you owe eighty-three thousand dollars in back taxes. I know your wife cheated on you with two men named Joseph and one named Daniel. And I know Malcolm succeeded in spite of your name, not because of it."

My brows shoot up.

Damn.

The announcers are calling for the start of my heat, but I can't leave, not when my father's hands are balling into fists and his bloodshot eyes are blackening with rage.

He glances over at me as I stalk up on Ryan's right, and his mouth opens and closes a few times before he finally sputters out his response and closes the distance between them. "Fuck you."

Ryan's only reaction is the lift of her brow, and I'm both impressed with her boldness and pissed at her lack of situational awareness.

"No thanks. I already know you'd be an inferior substitution for your son since your wife is still begging him to take her back." My jaw drops open as she licks her lips and smirks. "Want to know what else I know, Sullivan? I know you and Cara were already working together the day of Malcolm's accident. I know you made sure he saw you two fucking around when he hit the water. And I know that wasn't his board he was riding when he went down."

All I can say is thank God for sloppy drunks and best friends, because although I'm ready to take the brunt of Billy's fury at my back when he lunges at Ryan, it's Jeremiah who takes my dad down and shoves his face into the sand while I swing Ryan out of the way.

"It's go time, dumbass." Jeremiah grunts as two security guards rip through the crowd of spectators. He waits until Billy is subdued, then rises to his feet and points at Ryan. "Stay."

On that command, Jeremiah shoves me toward the tent where my board is propped and ready for me to kick some ass.

Chapter Twenty-Two

Ryan

"That's it," I whisper, unable to blink for fear of missing a single moment. "Go, go, go, go, go."

Wade is significantly louder beside me while he hollers advice in his grizzled voice until Malcolm rides the last of the wave's power into the shallow water to the sound of the spectators' cheers. "Better."

I'm straining to listen to the announcers above the din. I may still hold a grudge against them, and I can't understand most of their technical analysis, but their commentary tells me I'm not the only one who thinks Malcolm nailed it.

"This is the kind of skill we're used to seeing from Cole Sullivan, this absolute dedication to owning even the most uncooperative waves. What's your call on his shot at a win today, James?"

"I'd say there's no question, Garrett. Sullivan is back."

I can't contain my excitement as Malcolm exits the water with his board under his arm, joking and grinning alongside Jeremiah who rode in after him. Wade has gone stoic beside me, as though all his energy was drained from coaching his protégé from the sand. But he's a good sport when I grasp his arm and shake it, my smile dropping when Malcolm hands his board to

Jeremiah, changes course halfway to the competitors' tent, and beelines our way.

His expression is unreadable. All joviality is gone, replaced by a mask I can't decipher. My heart is pounding in my chest, either trying to get closer to him or warning me things are about to get very ugly and very public.

He stops in front of me, and his gaze sweeps from my head to my bare toes. "You're okay?"

"I am. Thank you." I swallow and squeeze the papers in my hands, which are becoming soft and damp from the combination of ocean air and my constant working of them. "You were amazing out there."

Glancing at Wade, he gives the man a nod, and Wade slaps him on the shoulder with a "good job, kid" before walking away, leaving no buffer between us.

I can hear people calling him back to the tent. The announcers haven't stopped breaking down each move he made on the water. Everything around us is swirling and vibrating and humming, but all I can see is him.

"You lied to me."

I blink back tears. "I did."

He nods and looks up to the sky for a moment before stepping in close and tilting my chin up. "Don't do it again."

His lips are soft as they brush against mine. Not hesitant, but gentle. Careful. My eyes flutter closed, and I sway into him as he breaks the kiss and rests his forehead against mine.

"I need to get back there for the score reading," he says quietly. "Come with me. We'll talk this out later, okay?"

I don't dare speak for fear I'll ruin this delicate

peace. He holds my hand while we walk to the tent, and he doesn't let go. Not when the scores are read. Not when he's pronounced the winner. Not until Jeremiah physically separates our fingers and the two men head to the podium to accept their trophies.

I gratefully fade into the background while he conducts interviews and poses for pictures. Fans stop him to congratulate him and welcome him back. Photographers swarm around the winners, calling out pose commands. The officials take turns speaking with him in hushed tones before smiling for the camera.

And through it all, he tracks me. I'm content in the corner, sipping a cold bottle of water and observing the excitement surrounding him. I feel a little silly giving him a thumbs-up every few minutes, but I don't want him to put an end to his impromptu comeback celebration.

Jeremiah extricates himself first, his second-place medal around his neck and slapping against his bare chest as he strides over and takes up position beside me. "You really fucked up bad, didn't you?"

Maybe his question should put me on the defensive, but it doesn't. Every word he spoke is the truth. "I did."

He cocks his head and crosses his arms, and I see such a resemblance between his mannerisms and Malcolm's that I have to bite back a smile.

"You get one chance. Mess with him like that again, and I'll spam every rating site out there with one-star reviews about your business. We clear?"

"Crystal."

Malcolm is frowning as he makes his way to us, and Jeremiah backs away, pointing to his eyes, then at me over and over until Malcolm swats at him.

"Ready to go?" he asks, using his board as a barrier between us and the people watching with interest.

Now that he's no longer distracted and riding the adrenaline rush, I find my confidence wavering with the intensity of his attention. All the rehearsing I did in my head on the drive here seems ridiculous, because for all my imaginings, I truly don't know how he'll take it. But I can't back out now. Nodding, I square my shoulders. "Ready."

"I need to swing by Barreled to see Emma first," he says as he takes my hand and leads the way out of the tent and through the thinning beach crowd to the lot where his truck is parked. "Then we can go out for a bite to eat unless you're okay with ordering in."

"Ordering in would be perfect."

I try not to read much into the way his fingers lace with mine or the kiss still ghosting across my lips. I'm prepared for today to be nothing more than closure for both of us. I don't dare think it may not be. Our ride is silent save for the music he puts on. A thickness is heavy in the air, a mix of uncertainty, questions, and answers hanging between us. But this isn't the time or place for the discussion we need to have, and we both know it.

Emma is sitting out front when we arrive, and Malcolm kneels down and talks with her while I hang back. She eyes me but doesn't say anything, and for that I'm grateful. With a kiss on her forehead, Malcolm hikes his board and motions to the stairs leading to his apartment.

****

Malcolm
I'm stalling.

Some might call it hiding, but technically, I did need

to shower, shave, and stare at my hazy reflection in the mirror until the steam evaporated. The fact I've been in my bathroom for forty-five minutes might look bad to an outsider, but it's my version of self-care before I go head-to-head with Ryan.

Am I a fool for hearing her out? Maybe.

Am I an idiot for thinking someone who deceived me for so long will be honest now? Possibly.

Am I opening myself up for a world of hurt I could avoid by kicking her out? Probably.

Does it matter?

Swiping my hand across the droplets dotting the mirror, I stare myself dead in the eye and accept my fool, idiot self.

"Was that the delivery guy?" I call as I exit the bathroom, knowing damn well our Chinese food has arrived because I can smell the black bean sauce.

Ryan is sitting at the counter, opening the multitude of boxes and shoving spoons into each. "This looks incredible."

I grab two plates and two bottles of water. "You don't live around here long without weeding out the good takeout from the bad."

She smiles, and while it may be hesitant and a bit reserved, my knees go a little weak.

Fuck, she's beautiful.

I hate myself for thinking it, because she's rocking the whole Adrian Dawson thing right now. Her tan stands out against the white fabric of her dress, and her legs look incredible with those heels she's still wearing. It's distracting and unnerving, and my mouth opens before my brains turns on. "You need to change."

The words hang in the air, but I can't take them

back. I can't do this with Adrian Dawson. I need to hash shit out with the Ryan I know without the constant reminder of who she really is.

She looks down, and I feel like a total ass when she frowns.

"Is there—"

I shake my head. "Forget I said anything. You look amazing. Gorgeous. I'm just being a dick."

Licking her lips, she stands. "Can I be honest?"

"That's kind of the point of all this, right?"

She takes a deep breath, which only makes the scooped neckline of her dress even harder to keep my eyes off. "I wasn't sure I was actually going to come to the competition today until I was there. I'm dressed for meetings with my lawyers, my realtor, and my accountant, not to eat Chinese and grovel. So if it wouldn't be overstepping—"

"You know where everything is," I reply without hesitation. "I'll get our plates prepped."

I should be uncomfortable with her in my bedroom going through my closet and drawers. I shouldn't be wondering if memories are assaulting her like they do every time I lie in my bed. I spoon out samples from each dish onto our plates and try to focus on why I'm willing to hear her out.

She knows things about the day of my accident.

She knows things about Cara and Billy.

She knows how much of us was truth and how much was a lie, and I can't let this—or her—go without knowing it, too.

I debate moving to the table but decide to stick with the counter. It's casual. Comfortable. Just like she looks when she walks in wearing my clothes.

My heart physically hurts to look at her, and I mentally kick my own ass for thinking this would make it easier.

She rakes her fingers through her hair, pulls it back into a ponytail, and hops up onto her stool. "Thank you so much. That dress didn't have enough room for me to gorge myself like I intend to right now."

I haven't seen this version of Ryan since we were together. Seeing her dressed in one of my old endorsement shirts and my favorite basketball shorts brings me back to coming home from my dawn training to see her sitting on her stool, a hot coffee in her hand and one set out for me. It felt so natural, like having her here now does. And it sucks because despite how easy she slips into my life, there's a chasm between us and I don't think I'll be able to jump it.

"I'm sorry," she states, and she takes a deep breath. "It isn't enough, and I know that, but I am."

Nodding, I don't speak. I don't trust my response. A small part of me wants to tell her it's okay, but it isn't.

She stares at her food for a moment, then looks over at me. "Can we eat this on the patio?"

"Sure."

She grabs her purse, and I lead her up the steps to the roof and move the chairs closer together so we aren't shouting to each other over the breeze.

We eat in silence for a few minutes until she points to the north strip of the boardwalk. "Do you see that woman?"

I follow her gaze to a female figure walking alone at a clipped pace, weaving past the slower movers on her way toward us. "Yeah."

"Her job is her entire life, and it has been for over a

decade," she says before she pauses to take another bite. "She works fourteen hour days. Her hobbies include checking her emails and color-coding her calendar. She lives alone above her office with no pets and no houseplants. Everything in her world is planned with contingencies and backups, and she leaves nothing to chance because she feels like she's one bad decision away from losing everything and she'll be back where she used to be—a nobody with nothing. Or worse, a nobody needing to rely on someone."

Swallowing the Kung Pao chicken, I sit back in my chair and pull my plate onto my lap. "Sounds tedious."

"She doesn't think so," Ryan continues.

I glance over to see her staring at the woman, her eyes glazed over.

"At least, she didn't. She grew up with a lot of unpleasant surprises, so for her, achieving this perfectly structured life is the ultimate success and her ticket to happiness."

"And is it working? Is she happy?"

Her lips purse. "Nope. Turns out some surfer dude with great hair and an incredible heart derailed everything. Which sucks for her, because she fell ridiculously hard for him, then screwed it all up, and she's been a wreck ever since because he was the only man she ever saw a future with, and now…it's gone."

We watch the woman disappear around the corner, and the time to play pretend comes to a screeching halt. I glance over to see Ryan picking at her food, swirling her fork around her noodles.

"Why'd you lie about who you are? I mean, I get why you did at first, but why did you keep it going for so long? It's just a name, Ryan."

"A name, a lifestyle, expectations, reality," she mutters, and she seems to shrink into herself. "Ryan was an old nickname from when I was a kid. Rose is my middle name. I'm your ex-wife two-point-oh version. I have money and yoga pants that cost more than most people's rent. I pretend to be someone I'm not every day. I'm eleven years older than you, and I represent everything you can't stand. Except when I was with you, I wasn't that woman. I could just be me because you didn't have any preconceived ideas about how I should act or speak or dress, and you were patient with me and nice without demanding anything in return, and you thought I was pretty without my makeup, and I didn't want to lose that, and everything kept snowballing—"

"Whoa," I interrupt, setting my plate down and turning to face her. "Did you seriously believe I would walk away from you because you're successful?"

She looks up at me with a stubborn tilt to her chin. "I was waiting for the right time to tell you."

"The right time would've been before you got mixed up with Billy," I growl. "How the fuck do you think it felt to have my asshole father introduce his date—*my girlfriend*—to me by her real name?"

The words hang in the air until she takes a deep breath and puts her plate beside mine. "If it was anything as horrible it felt to watch you leave the auction with Minda knowing what—" She swallows and shakes her head. "Never mind. I screwed up royally, Malcolm. And I'm so, so sorry. For lying to you about who I was, for going behind your back to knock your dad out of the running for Barreled, for not coming clean about any of it until my hand was forced."

We haven't even touched the iceberg we're crashing

into here, but I can't go farther with her thinking I slept with another woman. "Nothing happened between me and Minda," I say, wrinkling my nose when memories of that night assault me. "I got drunk, made a total fool out of myself, and talked about you until Jeremiah hauled my drunk ass home."

"She gave you five stars across the board, which boosted your rating by point zero one," Ryan replies before she winces. "I checked before we closed out your employee profile."

My lips twitch up in a half smile. "Stalker."

"You have no idea." She licks her lips and clasps her hands with a renewed resolve. "I should probably confess about Billy."

I hold up my hand. "If you fucked him, I don't want to know."

"Ew." She gasps with a shudder. "No. God, no. No, Malcolm. Just…no. I did fuck him over, though." She reaches down, pulls out the stack of folded papers she was holding at the beach, and passes them to me. "I needed to know where his finances sat, because I planned to go behind your back and make sure you didn't lose the bid. I pretended I was a huge fan of his and I wanted to come into Barreled as his partner. Except it was all for nothing." She shoves a strand of hair behind her ear while I unfold the documents. "He barely made the entry bid. You wouldn't have needed my help to win anyways."

I can feel my blood pressure rising along with my temper with her revelation. I've avoided thinking about Barreled all week, blocking it from my mind because I'm not ready to see the store and this apartment transfer into the hands of Billy Sullivan. Scanning the official-looking paperwork of a real estate transaction, I freeze. "This is in your name."

"Yup. In one month, I'll be your landlord."

"I—" I'm dumbfounded. Shocked. Confused. "What?"

Her knee is bouncing a mile a minute. "You backed out of the bidding because of me and my stupid plan to pull one over on Billy, so I took the first step to making this right. I outbid your dad, bought Barreled, and now I own a surf shop until I find someone to buy me out."

"Buy you—" I shake my head, trying to wrap my brain around everything. "Ryan, what the hell were you thinking? If you knew he couldn't afford much over the minimum, why did you pay double?"

She shrugs and looks at her pink-painted toenails. "I did a little digging into the sale and found out Wade and Emma need the money."

I'm torn. A huge part of me is awed and grateful on behalf of the couple who practically raised me. But I'm still pissed she did all this behind my back, so I focus on the least explosive issue. "You'll never recoup what you paid."

"I'm not looking to recoup. I'm looking to sell to the right person."

Chapter Twenty-Three

Ryan

Without the documents to hold, I have no idea what to do with my hands while Malcolm hunches over the papers and flips through them a second time.

"My board," he finally says, still averting his gaze. "What do you mean it wasn't my board I was riding that day?"

I knew this topic was coming, but it doesn't make it any easier, because no matter how much I try to cushion the blow or how long it's been, it's going to be tough for Malcolm to hear. "I needed to be a passable Billy Sullivan fangirl, so I studied and memorized his stats from every interview, article, and piece of video footage I could find," I open slowly as I twist the oversized T-shirt between my fingers. "I didn't go looking for the footage from your accident, but it came up as a link in one of the articles I was reading, and I couldn't resist."

He scoffs but doesn't look over.

"I didn't make it through the whole thing the first time. It took me three tries before I could watch to the end. But once I did—" My cheeks warm in embarrassment with the confession. "I studied the rest of your competition videos, and there was a subtle difference in the accident day from the start. Your foot placement was off. Your balance was a little wobbly.

You shuffled your feet around more."

Now I have his attention. He frowns and sits back in his chair, crossing his arms. "I would remember that."

"Not if you were already distracted," I counter. "There are a lot of amateur clips floating around if you know the right hashtags, and once I went down that rabbit hole, there wasn't a moment of that day leading up to your accident I haven't seen."

I reach into my purse, grab my phone, and pull up an email I sent myself once I put everything together. I tap the first video compilation I assembled and angle it toward him. "There you are on the bottom left. Something caught your eye, but you shook it off. In the next clip, you'll see your ex-wife using a surfboard as a shield to hide from you while she moves toward the competitors' tent."

The video plays out, and he restarts it. "I remember that. I saw someone with what I thought was my board, but when I looked over to the tent, mine was propped where I left it."

"It was," I continue, opening the next series of clips. "Until Cara traded it out. You can see her chatting with two of the judges who probably knew her through you. But right—here—she swaps them and passes your real board beneath the tent wall to Billy who disappears with it somewhere to the left of the screen."

He's silent while he plays and pauses the video time and again until he finally looks at me, his expression dark. "The replacement is six inches longer. I should have noticed."

"You noticed something," I point out, rewinding the moment he grabbed the board. "Check out your face. And the movement of your hand along the stringer."

He flexes his fingers, and his eyes glaze over. "There was damage. But I was late running into my heat and didn't have time to check it out."

I hesitate before showing him the last clip, the one I pulled from a small surf blog. Alone, it shows nothing Malcolm didn't already remember. But combined with the aerial footage of that day and Billy's own financial records, it explains more than Malcolm may want to know.

"Are you sure you want to see this?" I ask as I hover my thumb over the play button.

When he nods, his expression unreadable, I start it and stare out at the ocean without saying a word. I know every frame by heart. I don't need to see it again.

"At twenty-one seconds, you realized something was wrong. At twenty-five seconds, something caught your attention on the pier. Your board snaps at twenty-nine seconds, and you know the rest."

The video moves straight into the aerial, and anyone can see what caught Malcolm's eye. A beautiful blonde screams something from the nearby pier, and his head snaps to the side as Billy wraps his arms around the woman. But that isn't what sends him under. It's the break of his board beneath his feet immediately after that launches him into the unrelenting waves for ninety-seven seconds of heart-stopping fear.

He doesn't replay it. Or speak. Or move. He sits across from me with my phone in his hand without a single reaction.

"Malcolm? I know this isn't easy to—"

"But it is," he interrupts, shaking his head and taking a deep breath. "Seeing it laid out like this sucks, and I'm probably going to get real pissed eventually, but I'm not destroyed, Ryan."

Licking my lips, I decide to rip the last bandage off. "There's more."

He cocks a brow. "Great."

I ease my phone from his loose hold and open another attachment. "Billy's financial records indicate he started receiving large deposits shortly after you got married. A little deep-dive into his old social media account and I found your ex-wife, three years before you two met. Renna took it upon herself to confirm their marriage, sudden divorce, and remarriage through public records this morning."

He blinks.

His mouth opens and snaps shut.

He blinks again. "Well, fuck."

****

Malcolm

How the hell do I feel better knowing my ex and my own father conspired against me? I should feel like shit, but all I'm experiencing is surprise, a hint of annoyance, a tinge of stupidity, and relief it wasn't my own fuckup that nearly ended my surfing career.

I know Ryan is watching me like a hawk, maybe expecting me to freak out or yell or storm away. The nervous bounce to her knee has become faster and tighter like she's winding up for fight or flight, and all thoughts of Cara and Billy are swept aside as the need to reassure her I won't go ballistic moves to the forefront.

"Not gonna lie," I say, placing my hand on her knee to still it and damn near yanking my hand off when I can feel the spark we still have surging through me. "I'm more pissed about the money than I am about being played."

"I'm sorry," she says with a sigh, and her fingers graze mine before she slips her hands under her thighs. "I'm probably the last person you wanted to hear this from."

I grunt and pick up our plates as I stand. "It's getting cool. Let's head inside."

I'm stalling again, but avoidance is easier. I know I should thank her for the information, cross my fingers she won't raise my rent, and send her on her merry way, but I don't want to.

What I want is for her to stay and join me on the sofa for a movie and maybe catch a few highlights from today's competition reel. I want to hear her in my shower while I'm loading the dishwasher. I want her to get tired and rest her head on my lap and nudge my hand every time I stop playing with her hair. I want to carry her to bed and reacquaint myself with every inch of her body, and then I want to wake up to her curled up beside me.

Because as hurt as I was to discover she lied to me, being without her these past few weeks has been almost unbearable.

She follows me down the stairs silently and detours to my bedroom when I head toward the kitchen. "Thanks for letting me borrow these. I'll be a moment, then I'll get out of your hair."

No.

No, no, no.

Unless she really wants to go. Maybe she found someone else. Maybe she needed the closure on us to move on. Maybe she realized I wasn't worth risking her perfectly constructed world for.

Fuck, I'm a mess.

I'm knocking on my bedroom door before I can

think twice. "Ryan?"

She opens the door, and I grip the top of the frame to keep my hands where they belong when I see she's already taken off the shorts.

"Everything okay?"

"Yeah. No. I don't know." I exhale and shake my hair out of my eyes. "Am I that one bad decision that's going to wreck your life?"

"What? Of course not. I—"

"I love you," I blurt out. "All that shit you told me about Billy and Cara? I should be pissed, but I'm not because nothing is ever going to hurt as bad as losing you. My ex-wife left me for my own father who she was married to for years—who she was probably fucking behind my back—to leave me broke as hell and I. Don't. Care. I don't. What I do care about is how much I missed you, how much I hated waking up without you every morning, and how empty the rest of my life is without you in it."

I lower my hands and take a step inside. "You lied to me. But I get it. I don't like it, and I hope to hell you don't do it again. But if things had been reversed, I'd probably do the same because I love you, and if you love me even half as much, I get it."

Her eyes are welling up, and it breaks my heart all over again as she closes the distance between us and buries her face in my chest. I wrap my arms around her, and it feels so fucking right, like my universe is back on its axis.

"I never wanted to hurt you," she whimpers into my shirt. "I just love you so much it's terrifying."

I tilt her chin up and kiss her. Her lips are soft and familiar, and I try to keep it gentle, but when her fingers slide into my hair and she opens her mouth to me, all bets are off. I'm rock hard, clumsy, and desperate to bury myself inside her, and she's no more controlled than I am. She strips faster than I do and drags me down to the bed on top of her. Her nails dig into my biceps as I slip two fingers inside her to get her ready for me.

"I want your cock, not your hand." She groans, gasping when I oblige in one punishing thrust. "Like that."

I pound into her with the finesse of a jackhammer, and it isn't pretty. I'm grunting and cursing up a storm, and she's meeting every snap of my hips, moaning and pushing against my headboard for leverage. I feel almost feral with the need to reclaim her as mine, and while guilt over marking her so thoroughly might rear up in the morning, I can't resist the urge to bite and lick and nip at every inch of her.

"Don't stop, don't stop, don't stop," she chants.

I grab her hands from the headboard to hold them above her head as she tightens around me.

"Oh God, yes!"

Watching and feeling Ryan come undone sends me over the edge without warning. My toes curl, and my foot cramps, but the pain does nothing to detract from the sensation of coming inside her again. She's practically purring and trailing her fingers along the back of my neck by the time my senses come online again, and I roll off her, dragging her on top of me.

"You fuck like you surf." She sighs, her body draped over mine. "Like a champion."

I grin like an idiot. "Seriously?"

"Seriously." Propping herself up on her elbow, she looks at me, studying me long and hard and with enough intensity to make me a little worried about where her head is. "I really am sorry, Malcolm."

"Enough." I flip her onto her back, and my body immediately begins gearing up for round two. "We're going to talk tomorrow, we're going to argue a few times, we're definitely going to address this age hangup you've been hiding from me, but then we're going to have more makeup sex and figure us out, okay?"

She bites her lip as I rock my hips against her. "Okay."

Chapter Twenty-Four

Ryan

This is fine. Completely fine.

Malcolm is already making buddies with the daytime doorman, Ricky, while I pretend to hunt through my purse for my keys, so everything is most definitely fine.

"Let me get that for you, Ms. Dawson," Ricky says, breaking away from his conversation to unlock the elevator access to the penthouse. "There you are. If you can't find your key when you get upstairs, ring me and I'll have another cut for you immediately."

I give him what I hope passes for a grateful smile while Malcolm holds the doors open for us. "Thank you."

"Anytime, Ms. Dawson." He looks over my shoulder. "Hope to see you take the top spot at Mavericks in two weeks, Cole."

I follow Malcolm into the elevator, and the doors slide shut. "I didn't realize Ricky was a surfing fan."

"The biggest," he replies. "Good thing, too. He gave me quite the grilling before he realized who I was."

"Maybe we should go back down and register you as an approved visitor," I suggest, watching the numbers light up one by one. "Like, now."

He smirks and shakes his head. "Later."

"We might forget later."

"Are you stalling, Ms. Dawson?"

"Kind of," I admit.

He wraps his arm around me and kisses my forehead. "Unless you have a husband hiding in there, I'm pretty sure I can handle whatever you're worried about."

The elevator comes to a stop, and I let out a long-suffering sigh as the doors slide open. "I'm just not sure how messy it is and—"

He steps out into my impeccably clean entranceway. "Damn."

I try to see my home through his eyes, and it doesn't take much effort.

I know how it looks.

He takes his time walking through the kitchen and opens a few empty drawers on his way to the living room where my built-in bookshelves display books arranged by height and spine color. He scans the generic art on the walls, his gaze lingering on the piece above the electric fireplace where a TV should be.

"I'm going to shower," I say as I slip past him. "Make yourself at home, and I'll be out quick."

Nodding, he continues his perusal of the virtual show home I inhabit.

I try to track his movements over the running water but lose him somewhere in the vicinity of my office where he'll find nothing more than a desk, a laptop, and a metallic painting that came with the suite when it was staged for presentation the day I bought the property.

I rush through my routine, then wrap one towel around my hair and another around my body before I enter my bedroom to dress only to find him lying on my bed with his hands tucked under his head.

"Never in my life have I ever wanted to dirty something up so bad."

I open my lingerie drawer, select a deep-plum matching bra-and-thong set, and place them on my dresser before I cross over to my closet to choose a simple A-line skirt and black tank top. "I know it's a little barren—"

"Barren?" he echoes, sitting up and watching intently as I drop my towel and reach for my bra. "Don't get me wrong, this place is incredible. It's gorgeous. And it's so fucking staged I'm half-waiting for a real estate broker to walk in here and give me hell for lying on the bed."

Shrugging, I shimmy into my thong. "I'm not here much, so I haven't gotten around to making it mine."

"You literally work on the floor beneath us."

I feel more exposed with him taking in the nondescript light-gray walls and ornate crown molding than I do standing here almost naked. My home is cold. Impersonal. There's nothing indicating I live here. Unlike his apartment, which is filled with color and photos and paintings in mismatched frames, mine is decorated for display, for architectural and structural appeal. There isn't a single photo, no color except whatever the artists deemed necessary for the generic art strategically placed on the walls.

I don't even own a fake plant.

"When did you buy it?"

I wince and pick up my shirt. "Six years ago. But it's been a busy six years."

He's on me in a heartbeat, pulling me toward the bed and nuzzling my neck while he unclasps my bra with one hand and tugs on the lace band of my thong with the other. "I don't like thinking about you alone here."

I laugh at the ridiculousness of his statement as I straddle him. "I have top-of-the-line security."

He tucks my hair behind my ears and stares up at me. "Pack a bag. A big one."

****

Malcolm

I can't take my eyes off Ryan while she sits beside Emma on the sofa in the back room and laughs over stories about my childhood.

Wade interjects with his memories of the morning nine-year-old me was brought to the shop by two cops, buck naked except for a police jacket wrapped around me and zipped tight to avoid any more accidental exposures.

"In my defense," I call out across the room from my position at the card table where Wade and I are doing our best to polish off a plate of extra-hot wings, "I needed to test my theory that my board shorts were causing wind resistance while I was in the curl. It was research."

"It was mortifying," Emma retorts, turning to Ryan. "It was even more mortifying when he was brought here in the same state at three in the morning when he was twenty-one."

Refusing to go down without a fight, I lick the sauce from my thumb. "It was a dare. Blame Jeremiah."

Emma huffs, and Ryan smiles, and I'm happy.

She belongs here, surrounded by color and music and laughter instead of hidden away in some perfect mausoleum. Not even a quick roll on her crisp, white bedding could erase the sterility of her home from my mind, and I admit it bothered me more than it probably should.

I was shocked by Adrian Dawson's home. The fridge was filled with neatly stacked single-course meals and bottles of water set in perfect rows. Her cupboards had no open cereal boxes or cans of vegetables bought with the intention to eat but never actually used. Even her bathroom was void of any hint of her existence, her toothbrush hidden away in a drawer and her lotions tucked neatly behind the vanity mirrors.

Seeing her home made me understand her deception a little more. Nothing was out of place in her world, and everything was aligned to be appealing, effective, and devoid of any self-expression. Hell, she lived in the same building she worked in, and the two parts of her life had zero divide. Her closet held the only color in her home, and it was there where I had a glimpse of how that piece of Ryan shone through the Adrian Dawson she presented to the world.

Wade finishes the last of the wings and pushes the plate away as he leans in close to me. "Please tell me that woman of yours is bringing you in with her to run this place."

I shrug. "We haven't had time to discuss it. I don't expect her to."

His gaze moves to Emma, then Ryan, then back to me. "Did she tell you how much she overpaid? I'm a little concerned she might not have a good business sense."

"I'm sure she'll get the hang of it," I say with a chuckle, ignoring the memory of her saying she was aiming to sell. "She's a quick learner, I'll be around if she has any questions, and she does own a multimillion-dollar business and eleven commercial properties around the city, so I think she'll pick it up fast."

Wade's brows shoot up. "You got yourself a sugar momma."

"I heard that," Ryan calls over. "Watch it, Wade. Emma and I are discussing your retirement, and you don't want me filling her head with ideas, do you?"

Emma cackles, and Wade hunches forward, dropping his voice to a low murmur. "I used to think it would be nice for you to bring a good woman around, someone who Emma could spend time with. I don't think it's nice anymore."

Emma starts to tire soon after, and Ryan and I head out with promises to come back together so Wade can walk her through some of the finer details of running the best surf shop on the boardwalk. Ryan's cheeks are flushed, and she's smiling and relaxed as we take the stairs up to my apartment.

"Can we hit the water tomorrow before I have to head in to work?" she asks while she slips her shoes off and sets them on my shoe rack. "I brought my wetsuit."

"You bet we can." I take her hand and lead her to the living room where I proceed to pull her onto my lap as I sit. "What does the rest of your week look like?"

"Full," she states, reaching into her back pocket for her phone and tapping on her calendar. "Mildly full, actually."

"What exactly does mildly full mean?"

She licks her lips and twists her shirt between her fingers. "Renna convinced me to hire two managers to help oversee a lot of the day-to-day operations of Doll Parts, and I kind of agreed under duress in the form of a complete emotional breakdown on my office floor. So while I have to train them, I'm also relinquishing a lot of minor appointments, correspondence, and paperwork."

I wrap my arms around her and inhale the scent of her shampoo. "I don't like thinking about you being upset, but if it means you have help now, I'm all for it."

"Well, I do have another business to run," she replies. "Unless you know someone in the market for a surf shop. Someone who might want to go in with me and maybe run it together."

Leaning a fraction away from her, I frown. "What are you saying? You want me to buy in with you?"

She straddles my hips and places her palms on my chest. "The only reason I own Barreled is because there was no way in hell I was going to let Billy Fucking Sullivan get his cheating, stealing, nasty little paws on it. I can do the books, the advertising, and the ordering, but you know the place, Malcolm. You know the clientele and the culture. You're the only surfer Barreled sponsors—or ever has sponsored. If you want to buy in out of some misplaced equality bullshit, fine, but as far as I'm concerned, Barreled is mine in name only, which is why I had my lawyers draw up paperwork naming you as fifty-percent owner if you want it."

"I—"

"There's one catch," she continues, and her knee begins to bounce nervously against my thigh. "This apartment."

I'm not keeping up with her in the slightest. "What about it?"

"I like it better than mine, so I want to own fifty percent of this in exchange for fifty percent of Barreled."

I know I'm gaping like a fish, but I can't help it.

Two days ago, I had no Ryan and no Barreled. Now she's offering me both the business and— "You want to move in with me?"

"When you're ready," she rushes. She might actually be more flustered than I am. "If you're ready. Whenever you're ready if it happens to seem like something you'd want."

I stare past her shoulder at my flat-screen TV as everything clicks into place. "So tomorrow, then?"

Epilogue

Ryan

Two Months Later

Bindy and Yolanda are hot on my heels as I rattle off the must-do list for the weekend.

"I want two drivers on standby in case Jamie or Cullen run into issues trying to find parking for the concert, and make sure both have linked their phones up to the alternative phone number option Brit added to the app so they can make contact with their dates if they're running late."

Bindy's thumbs are flying across her screen while Yolanda fills her day timer with her delicate handwriting.

"We have full bookings for every employee slot from Thursday to Sunday afternoon, so alert me of any cancellations, because the waitlist is long." I pause to give them time to catch up as we enter my office. "Lastly, I'll be unreachable Saturday morning from seven until eleven, later if there's any deviation from the schedule. Renna is aware and will have her phone on standby."

My bags are sitting beside my desk, and the sight of them makes me both anxious and excited despite the fact they look…fuller.

Renna emerges from my bathroom and gives me a smile I know I don't trust. "Ready to go?"

"That depends," I say slowly, eyeing my suitcase and purse. "What have you done?"

She extends the handle on my luggage and steps back. "Nothing you won't be thanking me for Monday morning. Now go. Your stallion awaits."

As much as I want to stop and empty everything onto the floor, I know she's right because my calendar just chimed with a reminder.

I turn to Bindy and Yolanda, but both women are standing with their arms crossed and matching don't-even-think-about-it looks on their faces.

"Fine," I huff, dragging my suitcase out of the office. "I'm going."

"Not fast enough," Malcolm calls from the elevator as the doors slide open. "Come on, boss. We have a seven-hour drive ahead of us, and we still need to check in on Abby."

"And the contractor," I remind him, not too concerned about Barreled's newest employee but definitely on edge about the man in charge of turning our apartment into a masterpiece. "I think he's planning to install the darker flooring even though I was explicit about wanting the birch." Another thought occurs to me, and I stop cold. "Yolanda? Did we submit those landscaping receipts for the planter boxes out front? And we should start looking at our options for the Christmas party centerpieces before we're stuck with those dick flowers again."

He takes my suitcase and ushers me into the elevator as he waves to the women watching us with amused expressions. "Good luck this weekend, ladies."

"You, too, surfer boy," Renna calls back. "Don't choke and embarrass us all."

Before I can admonish her, the elevator doors close and I'm wrapped tight in Malcolm's arms, his lips on mine.

"Your vacation has officially begun," he states, his words muffled as he skims them along my neck. "Relax time starts now." He tips my chin and looks me dead in the eye. "You aren't alone. You have Renna, Bindy, Yolanda, Abby, and me all here, ready, willing, and capable of taking on all these details."

My shoulders drop. "You're right. I know you're right. But relax time starts once I see birch hardwood in our living room," I reply, sighing when my phone chimes. "Just a second."

I swipe my schedule open, read the latest update, and close out the app. "When did Renna give you access to my calendar?"

"When I told her you needed more sex time and less stressing-over-paint-chips time."

My eyes widen when I realize he's serious. "You didn't." I open the app again and scroll while he hefts my suitcase into his truck and opens the passenger door for me. "You did. Oh God, this is why Renna was so cheerful, isn't it? You gave her ammo, Malcolm. Ammo she'll use for weeks. Why would you do that to me?"

My color-coordinated schedule has a new shade of blue that fills every night with blocks of time in the early mornings and a few evenings. This weekend is completely cerulean with notes like *pre-competition lovin'*, *post-competition lovin'*, and *makeup sex*.

Frowning, I do up my seat belt and wait for him to get in. "Are you planning to fight?"

He taps my phone screen. "It's right there on the schedule. Friday, ten a.m. Argue over Malcolm accessing my calendar. And you'll see 'makeup sex' listed between the time we should be sending the contractor for lunch and when we hit the road."

****

Malcolm

I know there are athletes who swear abstinence makes them perform better in their sport, but I'm not one of them. If anything, I'm more focused on the water and hungrier for a win now that my dick isn't starving for attention and I have Ryan sitting on the beach waiting to celebrate another victory with me. After yesterday's makeup sex, last night's board romp, the christening of our hotel room, and this morning's quickie, I'm ready to get on my board, own the waves, and spend the rest of the weekend reminding Ryan there's more to life than being the Queen Bee CEO, ordering board wax, and bringing professional contractors to tears.

I'm also thinking a thank-you gift card for Renna is in order. Between the toys, the lingerie, and the stash of batteries she crammed into Ryan's suitcase, my imagination has been in overdrive for twelve hours solid.

My heat is called to the water, and I turn long enough to make a kissy face at her before I join the rest of the surfers aiming to take the top spot in the Mavericks' competition this year.

I hear Jeremiah taunting me from the beach as I paddle out, and I grin, knowing he's trying to throw my concentration so I don't obliterate his high scores from an earlier heat.

"Your woman thinks I'm hot," he calls, his voice loud and low with every vowel stretched out to the point of sounding ridiculous. "She calls me Big Boy."

I glance over my shoulder in time to see Ryan

saunter over to him with a bottle of water she tips onto his head, causing him to shriek before he bursts out laughing and slings his arm around her.

My knee still aches after long training sessions, and I'm not completely sold on the color Ryan chose for our living room, but my best friend and I are back on the circuit together, Emma and Wade are sitting on a beach in Barbados, Barreled is running smoothly, and the woman I love is cheering for me as I get into the pocket of a killer wave.

All I can hope for now is that she's looking good and hard when I go for an aerial, because I have a question for her written on the bottom of my board, and the sooner she says yes, the sooner I can convince her to sell our apartment to Jeremiah and start shopping for a home with more bedrooms.

A word about the author…

Katja Desjarlais is a music teacher by day and a paranormal romance writer by moonlight. She is an unapologetic music addict and has an obsession for bad Bach puns despite her irrational aversion to Baroque. Her favorite words include "plethora" and "dapper," and she is physically repulsed by the word "moist." Katja's interest in the paranormal can be traced to her early childhood film choices and to the revolving book collection on her phone.

Desjarlais lives in the Okanagan Valley with her husband, three children, and two black cats. Her ideal summer vacation is spent traipsing through the United States with her family and attending heavy metal concerts.

~*~

Find Katja Desjarlais online at:
katjadesjarlais.wordpress.com

Thank you for purchasing
this publication of The Wild Rose Press, Inc.

For questions or more information
contact us at
info@thewildrosepress.com.

The Wild Rose Press, Inc.
www.thewildrosepress.com